INFERNAL GOD

CLAIMED BY LUCIFER BOOK THREE

ELIZABETH BRIGGS

INFERNAL GOD (CLAIMED BY LUCIFER #3)

Copyright © 2021 by Elizabeth Briggs

All rights reserved. This book or any portion thereof may not be reproduced or used in any manner whatsoever without the express written permission of the publisher except for the use of brief quotations in a book review.

This is a work of fiction. Names, characters, businesses, places, events and incidents are either the products of the author's imagination or used in a fictitious manner. Any resemblance to actual persons, living or dead, or actual events is purely coincidental.

Cover designed by Sylvia Frost, thebookbrander.com

ISBN (paperback) 978-1-948456-09-8

ISBN (ebook) 978-1-948456-68-5

www.elizabethbriggs.net

1

LUCIFER

Heaven had once been beautiful. Now it was as desolate as my soul.

For months I'd been trapped here among the empty ruins of this once great civilization, under the sun that never truly set. Though I'd been born here thousands of years ago, living in Hell for so long had changed me. I desperately longed for night, for even one minute of complete darkness, but such a thing was not to be found in the Land of Light.

All I knew was a burning rage that simmered below my skin, fueling me in place of food or water or sleep. I needed none of those things now that I was an Elder God. I'd become War, second Horseman of the Apocalypse, and my purpose was to sow chaos and discord—as soon as I escaped. I had to find a way back to the human world to find the woman who had imprisoned me here. *To kill her.*

As I gazed across the shimmering ocean before me, I patted the neck of Strife, my one companion in this wretched place. The smell of brimstone and the sound of hoofs against the stone had become as familiar to me as breathing during our time here. Like me, my trusted steed required no sustenance, and no matter how hard or fast he ran, he never grew winded or fatigued. He'd simply appeared after I'd become War, and though he couldn't speak, we had a connection I didn't understand yet couldn't question. I was a Horseman, and Strife was my horse. It was that simple.

I nudged Strife across the white, gleaming sand toward the flowing waves. He moved faster than any horse, as fast as the sports cars I used to drive when I lived among the humans. Together we'd raced across Heaven for so long I'd lost track of the days as we searched for a thin spot between worlds. We'd checked all the places in Heaven that I knew had once been portals to the other realms, where I might be able to use my power to break through to Earth. All but one.

The Bermuda Triangle. Also known, rather fittingly, as the Devil's Triangle. There was a reason humans tended to go missing there. I hoped to exploit it.

White-hot rage burned in my gut as I pictured the woman who had trapped me here, and I squeezed Strife with my calves and heels, urging him to go faster, ride harder. Anything to get us out of this place so we could begin enacting our revenge.

Her alluring face had consumed my thoughts since the moment she'd disappeared through that portal, leaving me imprisoned in Heaven with Strife. I couldn't stop thinking about what I would do with her once I found her. I would bend her to my will, force her to her knees, make her pay for what she'd done. I would utterly destroy her. And then I would destroy her world.

Soon, war would spread across Earth, and then into all the other realms. Angels, demons, humans, fae—none would be spared my wrath, and all would bow to me. As it always should've been. As was my right.

I was the King of Demons. I was a Horseman of the Apocalypse. I was a *god*.

I urged Strife into the waves, where his hooves skimmed across the surface of the water. He could run over sea or land, desert or snow, it didn't matter. I spread my wings as we rushed across the dark blue ocean, enjoying the feel of the salt water on my skin and feathers. I held on with my knees and spread my arms, relishing in the power coursing through me. War had strengthened me, given me divine and righteous purpose. Nobody could stand against me. Not anymore.

After hours riding across the waves, I sensed something up ahead, a change in the air, a tingling sensation across my skin. We grew closer with every stride, and I wiped saltwater from my face for the thousandth time as I focused on the small island with an unmistakable magical signature.

Long ago, the realms of Heaven, Hell, and Faerie had permanent gateways open to Earth, and ancient monuments had been erected at the sites of them. When these gateways were closed, many of the locations became old ruins, like Stonehenge, or Chichen Itza. Others were lost in time, like the Hanging Gardens of Babylon or the Lighthouse of

Alexandria. This spot was one of the latter, an island that no longer existed on Earth, though it remained here in Heaven.

Using my knees, I urged Strife up onto the sand. Ancient stones of a once-great civilization loomed before me. This island had been abandoned long before Archangel Michael closed off Heaven permanently, and all that was left were a few crumbling pillars and stone walls covered in overgrown vines. Palm trees and lush green vegetation had taken over, but Strife had no problem finding a path through it until we found the center of the island. The large stones here formed a circle around a thin sliver of light, shining like a ray of pure sunshine, suspended in midair. Just a tiny tear in the veil between the worlds, but it was enough.

Strife pawed impatiently at the sandy dirt with his hoofs and blew fiery air out his nose. I felt it too. *Humanity.* Desperation and decay, with a strong tinge of passion and fear. The feel of their world beckoned me toward it. I'd found my way to Earth. Soon I would have my revenge, my glorious retribution.

I touched the sliver of light and pushed my power into it, drawing on the considerable reserves available to me as War. Old magic formed a barrier between the worlds, and I sliced through it, tearing the hole wider. Light burst through as I ripped the jagged portal open, until it was big enough to walk through.

Strife charged forward without hesitation and we passed through the portal. His hoofs splashed against the water as we emerged on Earth in the middle of the ocean, the island reclaimed by the dark depths of the sea long ago. I drew in a deep breath of crisp salty air, as the sun sank below the horizon and the sky darkened. Finally, the glorious night.

The stars and moon appeared overhead as Strife galloped forward across the dark blue waters. Toward my kingdom in Las Vegas. Toward the woman.

It was time to get my revenge and retake my throne. Then my apocalypse could begin.

2

HANNAH

Las Vegas heat was intense in May, but as an angel, I reveled in it. The warmth from the bright sun overhead was one of my few comforts these days. If I was being honest, life had been a bitch since I'd trapped Lucifer in Heaven. With War possessing him, he was safest there. I knew that, but I hated every second he was gone, and until I could find a way to save him from himself, I didn't see that changing anytime soon.

Six fucking months and still no sign of a solution. It didn't help that for the first three of those I'd done little more than sleep and puke my guts up. Morning sickness, afternoon sickness, evening sickness, all the damn time sickness, and my body didn't care that Lucifer was gone and someone had to step up to rule.

That person was me, of course. Pregnant, exhausted, heartbroken me. I'd barely managed to keep things together, but somehow I did it.

I became the Demon Queen.

With a lot of help from my friends. All of them pitched in during my time of need, going above and beyond in their efforts, and I couldn't have done it without them. Azazel protected me and kept me from losing my sanity. Samael and his assistant Einial ran the business side of things and kept the other Archdemons happy. Olivia and her angelic mates became my intermediaries with the angels, while my youngest son Kassiel helped me research everything I could about the Four Horsemen. They were all family—but they couldn't fill the void that Lucifer had left.

I took a deep breath and inhaled the floral scent around me from the other project that had kept me busy over the last few months—Persephone's Garden. The Celestial Resort and Casino's newest relaxation zone was almost ready to be revealed to the public in all its glory. There was nothing else like it on the Vegas Strip, a lush expanse of green with bursts of color forming a tranquil oasis in the middle of the desert city. Nature doing her thing with a little help from me. I'd included all my favorite plants, from olive trees and weeping figs, to lilies, violets, and irises. My favorite spot was a stone bench surrounded by Persephone's signature flower, the narcissus, better known as the daffodil.

There was only one last thing to complete—the magnificent waterfall. I moved along the path toward it, letting the fine spray soothe my heated skin. Once it was finished, the waterfall would become a gateway, allowing guests to walk underneath it to access other parts of the garden. The only thing unfinished was the secret cave behind it, which would not be for hotel guests, but possibly the most important thing I'd ever built.

Pride filled my chest. Lucifer had given me this space and I'd found my happy place in creating this garden over the past few months. I'd filled it with life and beauty, and although I could only just now bear the scent of some of the flowers, it was *my* place. Somewhere I could be fully me, with no demands on my time or my energy, where I could be alone with my tumultuous thoughts.

Or nearly alone. Even now, my ever-present gargoyle guard had fanned out into whatever pattern they'd determined would best protect me in this space. They weren't intrusive, but they were always nearby, usually in their human forms so as not to scare the hotel guests. Should any threat arise, they'd instantly sprout wings and talons, their skin turning to stone as they protected my life, and that of the precious cargo I carried.

The irony of it all didn't escape me. It wasn't all that long ago that I'd killed gargoyle after gargoyle in the penthouse when they'd attacked me, and now they were my biggest line of defense. How things had changed.

"Hannah," Azazel's voice called out from across the garden. She was near the lilies, and she carried their scent as she approached.

I stroked my hand idly over my bump and turned to face my best friend. As I did, my daughter kicked against me, and I smiled at the reminder of her presence. But then my smile faded as I wished Lucifer could be here for this, to experience her first movements and the joy she brought. I was nearly at the end of the second trimester. He'd already missed so much. I'd never even had a chance to tell him I was pregnant, let alone with a daughter.

"The Archdemons have gathered for the meeting," Azazel said. Her thick hair was braided down her back and her dark skin gleamed under the setting sun, though she squinted against it even in her sunglasses. The hour was later than I'd realized, and soon it would be dark. That was when the demons came out in Las Vegas. My demons.

I nodded but winced a little as my baby kicked again, this time right in the ribs. She was a strong one already. Much like the daughter we'd lost once before. Sometimes I wondered if this was the same soul come back to me, giving me a second chance to be her mother. There was no way to know of course, but the idea brought me a tiny bit of peace.

This time I wouldn't lose her. This time, if Adam tried to hurt her, I'd rip his fucking throat out. And this time, he'd stay dead.

Zel noticed me wince, and her hands immediately moved to her waist, the hilts of her daggers against her palms. "Is everything okay?"

Theo, the captain of my gargoyle guard, appeared beside us as if summoned by Zel's concern. He was tall and muscular, with black hair and a slight French accent, and his hands were already turning to claws. "Did you sense a threat?"

I shook my head and flashed them both a quick smile. By now I was used to them being overprotective, even if it could be annoying sometimes. "No, it's nothing. I'm fine."

Theo gave a cursory look around the garden anyway. "Let me know if you need anything, my queen."

"I will, thank you."

He bowed stiffly, then retreated again. Theo was the younger brother of Romana, the new gargoyle Archdemon. Their mother, Belphegor, had conspired against Lucifer in a plot to overthrow him, but Romana and Theo had chosen a different path after her death. They'd sworn loyalty to Lucifer, and now served me in his absence. A good thing too, because the gargoyles had proven to be the only people immune to Pestilence's plague attacks as long as they were in their stone form. That was one of the reasons Azazel had chosen them for my security. A smart move, since Pestilence aka Adam came for me three months ago.

It was hard to tell how much of him was Adam anymore versus Pestilence. They seemed to have merged into one horrid entity hellbent on destroying the world...and taking me as their prize. I supposed that meant there was still some of Adam left in there, which gave me hope for Lucifer too.

There was no way I was letting Adam take me, and I'd burn the whole world down before I let him hurt this baby. He'd already taken a daughter from me once, but never again. So when he came for me, as I knew he would, I was ready. My unusual mix of light and darkness powers had only grown stronger with my pregnancy, and my gargoyles and I managed to fight Adam off, weakening him enough that he had no chance but to turn tail and run. No one had seen him since.

Probably a good thing, since before his attack he'd been

making people sick all over the country. With Archangel Raphael's help, I'd formed a task force comprised of angelic healers and gargoyle warriors, who worked to clean up the chaos Pestilence caused. It was only a matter of time before he emerged again, and when he did, we would be ready. I glanced back at the waterfall, peering past the water at the cave behind it. A cave with a tomb inside it strong enough to hold an Elder God.

Or so we hoped.

3

HANNAH

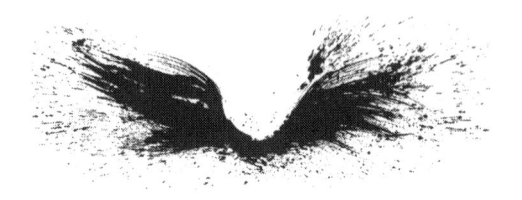

I walked, or perhaps slightly wobbled, into the meeting room with Zel at my side. I tried to appear cool, calm, and confident, hoping I looked like I knew what I was doing, even while my daughter continued to press against my ribs in the most uncomfortable way. Life didn't stop when you were pregnant, especially when you had a kingdom of demons to rule.

Samael was already there, along with the Archdemons Lilith, Baal, and Romana, to represent the Lilim, vampires, and gargoyles, respectively. I nodded to each of them as I took my seat at the head of the long table, but I couldn't ignore the fact that there should have been three more Archdemons present. The dragons were still staying away, remaining neutral after the death of their leader, Mammon. His son, Valefar, had not officially stepped up as Archdemon yet, and I suspected he was waiting to see what happened before he chose a side. The dragons' numbers were so low that I couldn't blame him for being cautious, even if I hoped he would join us.

The other two Archdemons, on the other hand, would not be welcome even if they came crawling back at this point. Nemesis, Archdemon of the imps, and Fenrir, Archdemon of the shifters, had gone too far in their attempts to overthrow Lucifer. They couldn't be forgiven for what they'd done. If it weren't for them, Pestilence and War wouldn't be released, and Lucifer would still be here. Of course, some of the blame also rested on my oldest son, Belial. He'd been the mastermind behind it all, at least at first, but I hadn't seen him since we'd trapped his father in Heaven. He appeared to have turned a corner at the end of that battle, as if he might have regretted acting against his father, but his continued absence troubled me. Now I wasn't sure where his loyalties lay.

Samael's dark eyes met mine in a silent question, asking if I was all right, asking if we could begin. He'd become indispensable to me in these last few months, a true friend I could depend on for anything, even though I knew he was hurting too. He wasn't one to show emotions, but Lucifer was his oldest friend, and he dearly missed him also. I gave him a slight inclination of my head, signaling I was ready.

Samael nodded to me and cleared his throat. "Now that our queen is here, we can begin. May I have everyone's attention?"

"You *always* have my attention," Lilith murmured as she gave him a little wink. As usual, she looked gorgeous with her dark curls and blood red lips, her green eyes accentuated by a low-cut dress of the same color. As the oldest succubus, she oozed sensuality even without trying, a perfect representative for the sin of lust.

Samael allowed his gaze to linger on her, but his eyes turned hard as they moved to her lover, the vampire Archdemon Baal. Samael and Lilith had been an item thousands of years ago, and so much history between them led to a lot of unresolved issues. Not least of which centered around their son, Asmodeus, and the fact Lilith had turned him mortal so he could be with my human friend, Brandy. I wasn't sure Samael would ever get over that, or accept that he would absolutely lose his son one day. Even so, it was impossible to ignore the way Samael and Lilith looked at each other, and as a succubus, Lilith needed more than one lover to keep her sated. I secretly hoped the two of them could work out their issues one day, but Samael was pretty damn hard-headed sometimes.

"Thank you for coming." I leveled my gaze at each of my Archdemons, who inclined their heads slightly in return. Even though I'd been born as an angel in this life, they'd all accepted me as their queen over these last few months, and I appreciated their loyalty. With their acceptance, the other demons had fallen in line too, and no one had questioned my position so far. "Has anyone learned anything regarding the whereabouts of Pestilence?"

Romana growled a little at the mention of the man who killed her mother. Like her brother, she had black hair, stony gray eyes, and a slight French accent, and she wore a skintight bodysuit. "No, nothing. My gargoyles have been searching for him, but he must be laying low and recovering his strength after his attack on you."

Zel leaned back in her chair and crossed her arms. "Do you think he plans to free Famine and Death next?"

"It's unclear what he wants, other than Hannah," Lilith said with a slight shake of her head.

"I've recently learned that Fenrir and Nemesis still plan to release the other Horsemen," Baal said, as he ran a hand through his long black hair. His British accent made me think of Lucifer with a pang in my chest, though Baal's was much more formal, to go with his antiquated black suit. Baal had been spying on the imps and the shifters for us, pretending to be their ally in this conflict, even though it was risky. "Though their attempt to overthrow Lucifer was thwarted when he became War, they've regrouped and decided on their next steps."

"What is their plan now?" I raised an eyebrow. Of course they had a plan B. I wouldn't have expected anything less from Nemesis and Fenrir.

Baal turned his icy blue eyes on me. "They're going to Faerie to release Famine in the hopes of taking you down. They have an issue with you becoming our queen, as you can probably imagine."

"No surprise there," I muttered.

"They'll have an issue with anyone sitting on the throne who isn't one of them," Zel said with a snort.

"Yes, and if somehow they did succeed, they would turn on each other next," Baal said. "They have no loyalty to each other either."

"Do you know if Belial is working with them?" I asked, though I was almost afraid to hear the answer.

Baal shook his head. "No, I haven't heard them speak of him lately. I don't think he's involved with them anymore."

That was a relief. Perhaps there was still some hope for my son.

Samael steepled his fingers. "We've already been working with High King Oberon to protect Famine's tomb in Faerie. Should Fenrir or Nemesis arrive in that realm, we'll be notified immediately."

"We must be prepared to do battle against not one, but potentially three Horsemen," Romana said with a slight growl. "And if the fourth one is freed, we are all doomed."

The thought of fighting Lucifer made my heart clench, but of course she was right. I had no idea if there was anything left of my mate in there now that War had possessed him, though I refused to give up hope. I pressed my hands against the table and addressed the others. "We're doing everything in our power to prevent that outcome. We have a tomb prepared to hold Pestilence, should he return here. War is trapped in Heaven, and all the keys to that realm have been hidden."

"What if he escapes?" Lilith asked softly, with a touch of sadness.

I swallowed hard. "I'll try to save him, however I can. And if I can't...then I'll stop him. Do not worry. I'll do whatever has to be done."

Silence fell upon the table as we all looked at each other with grave expressions. None of us wanted to take down

Lucifer, but we all knew it might have to be done to stop War. I'd been preparing myself for the horrible possibility for months now. Would I kill Lucifer if it was the only way to stop him? Yes. But I'd do everything in my power to find another way first.

The meeting closed out with more general demon issues, and when the Archdemons left, I breathed a sigh of relief and headed back to the penthouse to relax. As I entered, my first instinct was always to wonder what Lucifer would think of the changes I'd wrought in his absence. Nothing major, just a touch of my own style here and there. A few lush plants and more color, especially greens and blues, with comfortable pillows and throws draped across the furniture. It was a lot more soothing now, which both the baby and I desperately needed during these trying times.

I trailed my fingers over the fronds of a fern as I headed straight to the library. It had long been my favorite room, but now I glanced at the huge pile of books I'd been studying each night, and even my soul sighed. It was a mammoth task, but it was for Lucifer. For him, I'd do this every night for the rest of my life.

I opened my notebook and glanced at the latest I'd learned about the Elder Gods and the Four Horsemen. None of it seemed very hopeful. The Elder Gods couldn't be destroyed because they were ancient and primordial, representing basic components of the universe such as light and darkness, death and life. Just as one could never completely eliminate pestilence, war, famine, and death from the world, so too could those Elder Gods never be truly defeated. But they weren't all-powerful. For one thing, much like the fae, they couldn't lie. Of course, they were probably as tricky as fae too. Or even worse.

For another thing, outside of Void they required host bodies if they wanted to be corporeal. In addition, the Horsemen required a sacrifice from that host in exchange for giving them all the powers of a god, although I wasn't sure if that was true of all the Elder Gods. Pestilence required a sacrifice of the heart, which Adam had given when he'd killed his lover Belphegor. War needed a sacrifice of the mind, and it seemed he had taken Lucifer's memories of me as his payment. Famine supposedly asked for a sacrifice of the body, while Death needed a sacrifice of the soul—whatever that meant.

Not for the first time, regret and guilt squeezed my chest for trapping Lucifer in Heaven, but I'd had no other choice at the time. I couldn't let him come to Earth, not once I saw that War had taken over and turned my mate into someone else. Someone I didn't recognize...who didn't recognize me.

We were running out of options and out of time. At some point, we'd have to stop at least one of the Horsemen, if not all of them. We had the tomb in my garden, taken from Stonehenge and repurposed, but we weren't sure if it would truly hold an Elder God for long. It might contain Pestilence for some time, but what of the others? War was still out there, and Famine might be released soon. We might be able to defeat them—but if Death was released, I feared we would be completely screwed.

I flipped open one of the old tomes that described the

Elder Gods during the ancient times when all the different realms were connected. In those days, Elder Gods often fought and defeated each other. They couldn't be totally destroyed, but they could be subdued and removed from their hosts, which gave me some small amount of hope, although it was mixed with a heavy dash of terror.

I was starting to think the only way to save Lucifer was for one of us to take control of another Elder God. Of course, that would require a sacrifice, and there was no guarantee whoever did it would be strong enough to not be consumed by the god in the process. Or that they wouldn't need saving, once they too became a monster.

No, there had to be another way to get through to Lucifer. I just needed to keep reading through all these books, and surely I would find something. I had to.

I was the only one who could save Lucifer from himself.

I sighed and got up, stretching my aching body, then headed back into the main part of the penthouse and to the kitchen to grab myself something to eat. I had a feeling it would be a long night, and I was starving again. As I opened the fridge and began scanning the shelves, something caught my attention, something tugging against my soul, and I turned around.

With a boom that seemed to shake the entire building, the huge windows overlooking The Strip burst in, raining glass all over the penthouse. Instinctively I threw up a wall of darkness woven with light to protect myself from the blast, and when I lowered it, my mouth fell open. Framed between jagged shards of hanging glass was my mate, the person I most wanted and most dreaded to see.

I scrambled back toward the other side of the room, my voice trapped in my throat, preventing me from screaming for my guards. This couldn't be happening. It was too soon. We hadn't worked out a plan yet.

Lucifer's black wings spread wide, and anger and hatred burst out of his skin with an ominous red light, the same color as his eyes. Eyes that fixed on me with such fury it made my hands tremble and my pulse spike.

Lucifer had arrived—and he looked like he wanted to murder me.

4

LUCIFER

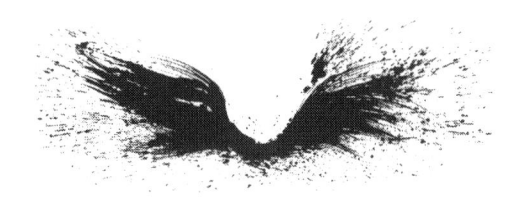

I roared, making the walls shake as I landed inside the penthouse. My throne room, now defiled by the blond woman in front of me. How dare she lay claim to my seat of power and then turn it into a fucking garden. Everywhere I turned, there were more flowers, and the air smelled of nature. I could almost hear the plants growing. Another reason to end her. Slowly. Painfully. While she begged for mercy on her knees.

"What the fuck do you think you're doing here?" I asked, as I stalked across the room. The pull toward her was irresistible, and I devoured the sight of her full hips, heaving breasts, and lush lips. I sensed her fear, and it was intoxicating. Damn right she should fear me. All living things should. "You locked me in Heaven and now you claim my home as your own?"

Even with terror coursing through her veins, she stood straighter, defiantly staring back at me with those magnetic blue eyes, while her hand lingered protectively over her belly. "No, Lucifer. I live here—with you. This is *our* home. Don't you remember?"

"Liar!" I yelled.

Her eyes widened like she knew what I was about to do before I conjured a sword made of hellfire and shadows. It was darkness wreathed in red fury, and power coursed through me when I held it over her. But as I looked down at her face, that beautiful face that had haunted me for months, my sword never fell. My grip tightened around it, but I couldn't deliver the killing blow.

Something stopped me from ending her. And worst of all, she knew it.

Instead of screaming in fear and running away, she stepped closer, so close I could smell her. Flowers, vanilla, and something else, something primal and all feminine that made my cock harden.

"Lucifer, put the sword away," she said. "Remember who you are. Remember *me*."

"I know exactly who I am," I growled. "And you will die."

"No, I won't. You can't kill me." She put her hands on my shoulders, and the sword I held vanished like smoke. "You won't."

I wrapped my hand around her throat, but my fingers wouldn't tighten. Instead my grip became more of a caress, and she sighed and closed her eyes. As if she *liked* it. How could she possibly crave my touch? And the more important question—why did I crave hers even more?

"Who are you, woman?"

She reached up and stroked my face tenderly, as she looked at me with something I didn't understand. Her touch was a bolt of electricity that stormed through me, lighting me up in a way the anger and the hatred didn't. "I'm Hannah, your mate. Your queen. From the dawn of time, we've been bound together by fate. You sacrificed your memories of me when you became War, but I know, deep down, the man I love is still in there."

She was wrong. I was Lucifer and War and there was no room for love in my wrathful heart. Especially not for an angel. Yet her touch stirred something in me, and my hand slid from her neck down to her breasts, while I watched her lips part with a soft gasp. At the sound, my other hand grabbed her hip possessively and pulled her against me, before I realized what I was doing.

Then she was in my arms and my mouth was on hers, my lips rough and demanding, crushing hers as I stole her breath. My tongue stroked the warm, wet softness of her mouth as I deepened the kiss further, backing her against the wall, one arm wrapped around her, one hand resting on her hip. Everything about kissing this woman felt right, and I couldn't get enough of her. From the way she kissed me back and clung to my shoulders, she felt it too. How?

I didn't know. Didn't care. I had to have her. My cock demanded to be sheathed inside of her, and I would pound her hard until I had answers. I nudged her legs wide, sliding a hand between her thighs, finding her wet and ready. She gasped and arched against me, and I let out a low hum of satisfaction. Soon I'd make her scream my name.

I ripped her loose dress down the front, exposing her bra and panties, but then I saw the fullness of her belly and paused.

Fuck. The woman was *pregnant*.

My hand came to rest across her abdomen and I felt the life growing inside of her. It called out to me, filling me with an unmistakable truth.

Mine.

The woman carried a life. And not just any child, but one my blood recognized as its own.

Impossible.

I stumbled back, forcing my eyes up to her face. "How?"

She looked almost sad as she stared back at me. "It's yours, Lucifer. But you know that, don't you?"

"It can't be. I would never breed with a filthy angel!"

She sighed and reached for me again, but I drew away. I couldn't trust her. I didn't know her. She was nothing to me. Yet somehow she carried my child within her. What. The. Fuck.

"You can fight this," she said, stepping closer to me. "Fight it for me. For your daughter. For us."

Daughter? I didn't know what she was talking about, but something wasn't right about this. Conflicting thoughts and emotions warred for control in me, making me unable to tell what was true or not. She had tricked me somehow, confusing my thoughts, and I had to get away to make sense of it all.

My wings snapped out and I let the familiar anger and

hatred fill me. Yes, that was better. That was real. That was *me*.

Without another glance, I launched myself out through the broken windows, the taste of her still on my lips. I couldn't kill the woman, not while she carried my child.

But I would return.

5

HANNAH

Damn, I almost got through to Lucifer.

I stared through the shattered windows where his red glowing wings had carried him into the night. He'd come here to kill me, I had no doubt about that, but he couldn't do it. Even though he didn't remember me, he'd felt the mate bond thrumming between us, pulling him toward me until it was impossible to resist. When he kissed me, I felt my Lucifer shining through, and I knew he wasn't all lost. He could still be saved—but I had to do it quickly before he started another war between angels and demons, or something worse, something I couldn't even fathom.

There was only one way—I'd have to use Famine to take War down.

The penthouse door burst open and Theo ran inside, followed by the other gargoyles in my guard. I hastily grabbed my ripped dress and tried to cover myself up, but my hands trembled and my heart pounded so loudly I could barely hear Theo's words.

"My queen, are you all right?" Theo had his sword out and he gripped my elbow protectively, ready to guard my body with his own while his gargoyles scoured the penthouse and took to the skies to search for the threat.

"I'm okay," I said, trying to pull myself together as I looked down at the glass all over the floor. Those poor windows had been replaced more times than I could count at this point. "I'm not injured. Just shaken, that's all."

"Who did this?" he asked.

I hesitated, but there was no hiding this from Theo or anyone else in my inner circle. "It was Lucifer."

Theo swore under his breath in French. "He escaped? Where did he go?"

"I don't know."

Azazel flew through the front window, a murderous look on her face. "I'm going to kill him," she muttered as she landed and her wings disappeared. She took one look at me in my ripped dress and narrowed her eyes. "What did he do?"

"Nothing. I'm fine." Lifting my still-shaking hand to my lips, I ignored the slight sting his rough kisses had produced. There was no denying how much his touch had turned me on, and that had a lot to do with why I was still trembling. I'd missed Lucifer so much over these last few months, and with these pregnancy hormones raging inside me, I'd been unable to stop my body from reacting to him. Even now, need pulsed between my thighs, begging for him to return and finish what we started.

Zel didn't look convinced. "The baby?"

I rubbed my bump and was rewarded with the familiar feeling of her rolling over. "She's fine too. He didn't hurt us. He never would."

Zel crossed her arms. "We don't know that for sure."

"We'll double our guards immediately," Theo said, his head bowed. "I apologize, my queen. This should never have happened. I'll investigate immediately why my gargoyles weren't here to defend you."

I waved his apology away. "As impressive as your guard is, I don't think any of them could have stopped Lucifer tonight. But I nearly got through to him, which means there is hope."

Zel's face softened. "Hannah, I know you think that, but—"

I held up a hand to stop her protest. "I *will* find a way to save him. Call a meeting immediately with all my advisors. We have a lot to discuss and only a short time to develop a plan."

Less than an hour later, I sat in a rocking chair Zel had turned up with one day for the nursery, which had once been my bedroom in the penthouse, and then my office. She'd given no explanation, but the chair was plush and comfortable, and I'd loved sitting in it ever since. It had been a sweet gesture on her part, and it was the only thing in this room so far. I hadn't decorated the nursery yet—mainly because I kept stupidly hoping Lucifer would do it with me. Maybe such hope was foolish, but I couldn't allow myself to give up on it. If I did, I would truly sink into despair, and I'd had enough of that already in all my lifetimes.

Zel poked her head in the door. "They're here."

I joined everyone in the dining area of the penthouse, which had been cleared of glass already, and sat at the head of the table with the people who had been willing to drop everything to rush to my side. Samael and Einial, of course, plus Azazel and Theo, along with my youngest son Kassiel, his mate Olivia, and her other men, Callan, Bastien, and Marcus. They'd become my inner circle over these past few months. "Thank you for coming on such short notice."

"What happened here?" Kassiel asked, his green eyes filled with worry as he took in the broken windows. Pride and love filled my chest when I looked at my youngest son, with a touch of grief because he resembled his father so much. Our youngest son was truly the best of both of us—smart, loyal, and brave, and always fighting for peace.

There was no sugarcoating what happened, so I simply said, "Lucifer has broken out of Heaven."

Many around the table gasped or widened their eyes in shock, but Samael simply asked, "How?"

"I don't know."

"What did he want?" Olivia asked.

I let out a weary sigh. "I think he wanted to kill me, but he couldn't do it. Even though he didn't remember me, he knew me on some level. When he discovered I was carrying his child, he seemed...confused. Or conflicted. Then he left."

"Any idea where he might go next?" Callan asked. He was a fierce angelic warrior and the son of my sister, Jophiel, who had died while protecting me from Pestilence. Since then, Callan and I had grown closer, clinging to what family we had left.

Bastien, another angel and always the logical one in the group, stroked his chin. "Considering last time he tried to reignite the war between angels and demons, I suspect wherever he's going, it won't be good."

"Don't forget he can also turn people into frenzied warriors," Marcus added, reminding me of those final moments in Heaven and the chaos Lucifer had caused. As a Malakim healer, Marcus had been one of the angels responsible for dealing with the aftermath of that fight.

"All the more reason he needs to be stopped immediately," Zel said.

Kassiel turned to her. "Or saved."

Zel scowled. "We'll see."

I pinched my brow, fighting off exhaustion. "Lucifer is a threat, there's no denying that. Before we do anything else, we need to warn Archangel Gabriel that Lucifer is back on Earth."

Einial spoke up for the first time. "I'll get right on that."

"Thank you." I nodded to her before continuing. "I don't know if there is a way to save Lucifer or not, but we're going to try. I did come across something in my research that has given me hope. We might be able to use another Elder God to subdue War and free Lucifer. Which means we need to go to Faerie immediately."

"You want to free Famine?" Kassiel asked, his eyes filling with horror.

"I do, yes. Before Nemesis and Fenrir do it first."

"No way," Callan slammed his hands on the table. "This is way too dangerous. Especially for you in your current state."

"It's the only option we have right now," I said. Callan had lost both his parents, and I understood that he couldn't bear the thought of losing me or his future cousin either. My nephew tended to be overprotective of those he loved anyway, but even so, he couldn't stop me from doing what I had to do. No one could. "If we release Famine ourselves, we can control the situation."

"But one of us will have to make a sacrifice to host Famine," Olivia said in a quiet voice.

"I'll do it," Kassiel said, and everyone else at the table chimed in offering their bodies instead. Warmth filled my chest, along with a heavy dose of sadness. There was so much love at this table. So much bravery. I couldn't bear to lose any of them either.

Zel rose to her feet. "It has to be me. I'm the oldest and strongest, and unlike the others here, I have nothing to lose." Her dark eyes turned to me, glimmering with both pain and determination. "You know it's true."

I pressed my lips together, but then nodded. Azazel was

a good choice, as much as I hated to admit it. She was one of the few who might be able to control the Elder God inside her, and unlike the others, she wasn't in a relationship. She'd lost her fated mate years ago, and as far as I could tell, she had never truly gotten over it. I wasn't sure she could.

But she was also my oldest and dearest friend, who had stood by my side for centuries, across hundreds of different lives. What if she became a monster like Lucifer? Would I have to stop her next?

The thought brought tears to my eyes, but I knew she was right too—it had to be her.

"It's decided then," I said. "Azazel will become Famine's host. Einial, please send a message to High King Oberon informing him we will need admittance to Faerie as soon as possible."

"I'm going with you," Kassiel said. "And we'll need to get Damien too."

My chest tightened at the thought of finally seeing my other son. I'd wanted to visit him in Faerie for months now, but it had never worked out with everything else going on. Now we needed him—Damien was one of the only people who could open Famine's tomb.

"Before you go, let me check on you," Marcus said, rising to his feet. "Are you sure you're not injured from Lucifer's attack?"

"I'm fine," I said, for what felt like the hundredth time. No one seemed to believe that Lucifer had never really been a threat to me. Or that I could take care of myself, even while pregnant.

"You should let him check you out, Mom," Kassiel said. "Or at least check the baby. We want to make sure you're both fit to travel to Faerie."

"Okay, okay." Yes, I was six months pregnant, but I was also an immortal being with Archangel blood and memories dating back thousands of years. I wasn't exactly fragile. But I knew their concern was only a sign of love, so I made myself let it go.

Marcus walked around the table to crouch beside me. I turned enough for him to put his hand on my bump, and a soft white glow emitted from his palms. "Your daughter is strong and powerful. Just like you."

"Thank you." I let out a slight sigh of relief. Not that I'd been worried, but after losing a daughter before, it was always a comfort to know this one was doing well.

"I should go with you too," Marcus said, as he stood up. "Just to be safe."

"No, I need you to stay here in case Pestilence returns," I said. "If he does, the people at this hotel will need your healing desperately. You'll remain, along with Olivia, Bastien, and Callan."

Callan jumped to his feet. "Fuck that. I'm coming with you. The others can stay, but you need at least one angel with you. That's my niece in there, after all."

I pressed my lips together, but then reluctantly nodded. I should have known he would be eager to go with me as soon as I told them my plan. "All right, and we'll take some of the gargoyles too. Samael and Einial, I need you to keep things running here while I'm gone."

"Of course," Samael said. "We'll be prepared in case Adam or Lucifer should return."

For their sake, I prayed that didn't happen, or I might not have a kingdom left once I returned from Faerie.

6

LUCIFER

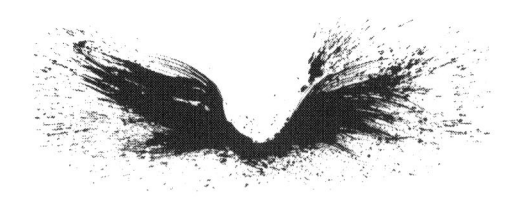

A thin sliver of moon hanging over California lit my way as I galloped toward Angel Peak, a small angel-only town where Archangel Gabriel currently resided. Like a fool, I'd once made peace with the angels, but War had shown me the error of my ways—and now it was time to start that ancient battle once again. It was eternal and endless, the conflict between light and dark, good and evil, day and night. It was not about the victor, but about the fight itself, and it must continue.

The angel woman, the one living among the demons and carrying my child, she wouldn't want war. Somehow I was certain of that. But what she wanted didn't matter. All that mattered was bringing the angels to their knees. Then the humans, and the fae after that.

Using my powers of darkness made concealing myself easy in the shadows of the night as Strife rocketed through towns, down highways, and over large swathes of land. It felt like no time at all before we stopped in the front yard of Gabriel's quaint little mountain home, situated near Seraphim Academy, where all the good little angel boys and girls went to school.

"Gabriel!" I thundered as Strife cantered around the house. "Show yourself!"

When I reached the back porch, I found him waiting for me. Gabriel was sipping a beer and seemed to be expecting me. With his sandy hair, faded jeans, and friendly face he looked like someone's favorite uncle, not the leader of all of angelkind.

"Hello, Lucifer," he said in a sad voice. A *weak* voice. "They told me you'd found a way out of Heaven. I wondered if you'd pay me a visit."

"We have unfinished business between the two of us." I jumped from Strife and he reared back with a loud squeal, then thundered away. He'd return when I needed him.

"You want a beer?" Gabriel asked, before holding one out to me.

I narrowed my eyes at him, wondering if this was some kind of trick. Did he think he could poison me? Or was his plan to make me drop my guard in the hopes of surprising me with an attack? Surely he knew that wouldn't work. "No, I don't want a fucking beer. I'm here to declare war against your people."

Gabriel let out a long sigh. "And here I thought we were friends."

"Friends?" I spat on the ground. "We've been enemies since the Elder Gods made us."

INFERNAL GOD   37

"That's not true and you know it. We were friends long ago in Heaven, before you turned your back on us and left for Hell. Sure, we had a few years where we didn't see eye to eye for a while and kept trying to kill each other, but then we became friends again after the war ended. Besides, our children are in love. That makes us family now."

"Children?" I bristled at that. "I have no children."

Gabriel whistled softly. "Damn, War's really done a number on your head, hasn't he? It's bad enough he made you forget Hannah, but to forget your own sons...that's truly evil."

Sons. Plural. How was that possible? How could I not remember any of that? Something wasn't right. Something big was missing from my past, and I needed it back. I raged inside, fighting at War's hold as I searched for answers, but he was too strong. The anger overtook me again and all I knew was fury.

"Enough of your lies!" The sky had begun to turn purple near the horizon, a sign of the coming dawn. With War inside me, I had no fear of being overpowered by Gabriel, but I wanted to get this over with already. I forged my sword of hellfire and shadow and pointed it at the Archangel. "As King of Demons, I declare war against the angels. Prepare your people for battle."

Gabriel rose to his feet and his silvery wings spread out behind him. "I cannot do that, Lucifer. You know I would never willingly send my people to war against the demons again. Just like you would never go to war against us again if you were in your right mind. We both know what it cost us last time. We lost Heaven and Hell, and for what? Our pride?"

Fury coursed through me as I raised the sword. "If the angels won't fight willingly, then I'll make them. I'll destroy your towns. Your schools. Your homes. War will come to your people, and once I slaughter everyone they love, they'll have no choice but to fight back—or surrender like the cowards they are." Hatred for this angel who thought himself good and pure tightened my chest. In reality, he was spineless, unable to win a war he'd fought for a millennia. Now he tried to trick and taunt me with his words of deception and peace. Friends? How could I possibly be friends with one such as him? "But first, you will bow."

Walking forward, I released my War powers toward Gabriel, sending my rage into his own mind. Gabriel was strong, probably one of the strongest minds I'd ever encountered, but I'd controlled him before, and I could do it again. And after a few minutes of struggling, even the mighty Archangel Gabriel gave in.

Weak. Pathetic. Like all the angels were.

No, not all of them. The woman who'd locked me in Heaven wasn't weak. She'd fought back against me. And now that she carried my child inside her she would only be stronger.

I forced all thoughts of her from my mind as I fueled rage into Gabriel, until his eyes and wings glowed with red light. His face filled with hatred as he looked upon me, and I knew if I released him, he'd go for my throat.

"The angels will prepare for war," he said. "Where shall we begin the battle?"

"In Las Vegas." It was the seat of demon power here on Earth, and if we took out some humans at the same time, even better. The woman was also there, but I'd deal with her. Somehow.

The Great War was beginning again, and soon it would consume the entire world.

7

HANNAH

I woke early the next day, adrenaline already coursing through my blood. Lucifer had forced our hand with his escape, but I was ready to rescue him. I had a plan now. Would it work? I had no clue. But I didn't have any other ideas, and we had to try something. I couldn't let my husband remain a monster any longer...or let him destroy this world and every other one.

I fluttered about the penthouse as I got everything ready, ate a healthy breakfast, and then went to don some battle gear for whatever we might face. Except maternity stores didn't exactly make armor for pregnant angels, so I settled for comfortable clothes I could easily move in instead. If everything went well, there should be no need to fight, but it was best to be prepared for the worst in situations like these.

I headed out to Persephone's Garden with a thick circle of gargoyle warriors around me. The attack from Lucifer had shamed them, though I'd learned that Lucifer had used his War powers to cloud and confuse their minds. They'd never stood a chance against him anyway—better for everyone that they'd stayed away. Even so, Theo had been extra vigilant ever since, and I feared I'd never get a moment of privacy again.

When I arrived at my favorite bench, I was shocked to find someone else sitting on it—Belial. My eldest son wore a black t-shirt that showed off his muscles and tattoos, along with dark faded jeans and combat boots. If you didn't know better you might mistake him for his father, except Lucifer would never be caught dead in that outfit.

He stood when I approached, and my guard immediately surrounded him with swords and claws, some quickly shifting to their gargoyle forms. Belial looked unfazed by it all and didn't even bother to unsheath Morningstar, the sword strapped to his back that had once been his father's.

I rushed forward and belted out a command. "Stop! That's my son!"

"He's a traitor," Theo said, narrowing his eyes at Belial. "He's a *threat*."

"He's not a threat to me." I waved them off, and the gargoyles reluctantly lowered their weapons and backed away. I moved closer to my son and took him in. "What are you doing here? Where have you been?"

"You're looking good, Mother," Belial said, his eyes dropping briefly to my stomach. Then he looked at me again with a challenge in his gaze. "I heard you're going to Faerie. I'm coming too."

"How did you hear that?" I bristled, wondering if we had

a spy in our midst. Belial clearly had been keeping tabs on me since he didn't seem surprised by my pregnancy, and he knew to be here at exactly the time of our departure. Someone was giving him information. Who was it—Samael? Einial? Definitely not Azazel, she hated him...

He gave a small shrug. "I have my ways."

Stubborn child. I bet it was Kassiel. They were brothers, after all.

I sighed and crossed my arms. "Why do you even want to come? How do we know we can trust you?"

Belial's jaw clenched. "It's because of me that Pestilence is freed, and I planned to make it right by becoming War and taking Adam down. Father ruined that, and now he needs saving too. If you're going to use Famine to fight him, I want to be there."

"What of Nemesis and Fenrir?"

"I'm not working with them anymore."

His words rang with truth, and I checked his aura and saw no other hidden lies or deceptions there. I nodded slowly, knowing the others wouldn't like it, but unable to deny how relieved I was to see my son again. He'd made a mistake—okay, a hell of a lot of mistakes. But he was still my son and I would always give him another chance.

I was about to tell him he could come with us, when Azazel rounded the corner with Callan and Kassiel. They were dressed for battle, and Zel let out a shout and rushed forward at the sight of Belial, daggers in hand. Callan growled and charged too, and this time Belial began reaching for Morningstar. Only Kassiel's quick movements blocked them before a fight broke out, his body moving to shield his brother from harm.

"What is *he* doing here?" Zel asked, her dark eyes flashing with anger.

I stood beside Kassiel in front of Belial. "He's coming with us."

Callan shook his head. "No way."

"I have to agree, my queen," Theo said. "My official position is also no."

"We should give him a chance," Kassiel said, his voice still calm and steady. Yes, it was definitely him who'd brought Belial here. They'd probably been talking for months, and though I was annoyed that Kassiel hadn't told me, I had to respect his loyalty to his brother.

"How can we trust him?" Callan asked.

"He spoke the truth when I questioned him." I cast a firm look at everyone standing before me, and channeled my authority as queen into my voice. "Belial's coming. That's my final decision."

Theo stiffly bowed, Callan scowled but nodded, and Zel regarded me with a stony expression, but in the end even she inclined her head. Belial just stood there with his arms crossed like he didn't give a damn about what was going on. A lie, of course. Though he might fool others with his uncaring facade, I knew his heart was in the right place and that he actually cared more than he would ever say.

As they all put their weapons away, Einial entered the

garden with a woman with burnt orange streaks in her black hair, which was tied back to show off her pointed ears.

"This is Mirabella," Einial said. "One of our messengers to Faerie. She's half-Fallen, half-fae of the Autumn Court."

Mirabella dropped to a deep curtsy before me. "My queen, I'll be opening the portal to Faerie."

"Thank you," I told her. "Can you do it from here?"

She straightened up and nodded. "Time and space are different in that realm, so you don't need to go to a particular place before you cross over—all I have to do is focus on the destination, and the portal will take us there."

"Convenient," I said.

"I'll take you as close to High King Oberon's palace as I can. Are you ready, or do you need more time?"

I glanced at my companions briefly, but none of them had any protests. We were all here, and there was no reason to delay. "We're ready."

She nodded and removed a small gemstone from her pocket. It was similar to the one I'd used to open Heaven, but this one swirled with a rainbow of colors, all constantly shifting and changing in a pattern that was mesmerizing. She held it out before her and the colors shot out in a beam and formed a glowing portal, large enough for all of us to pass through. Einial stepped back, since she would be staying behind, while Theo and some of his soldiers went through first to ensure it was safe.

Once they'd determined there was no threat, I walked through the portal, discovering another world, one of nature and color and the heady perfume of flowers. A light spring rain fell upon us, and if I remembered correctly, that meant it was morning here also. Faerie was unique in that it went through every season over a twenty-four hour period, from blazing hot summer days to bitter cold winter nights.

We stood in the middle of a courtyard surrounded by white pillars wrapped in dark green ivy, and I looked up at the sky, so blue it almost sparkled like the ocean. To my surprise, Faerie felt like home, just like Heaven had. I breathed in the scents that drifted tantalizingly from the oversized blooms that grew up around us, and something woke inside me, unfurling and stretching, taking over.

Power.

I spread my fingers and tiny white flowers appeared before them, sprouting up from the dirt and grass at our feet, growing faster than was possible in nature. A strong breeze picked up, toying with the blades of grass, making the flowers dance, and I let out a bright laugh. As Persephone, I had been a princess of the Spring Court—and my powers had returned.

"What was that?" Callan asked.

"When Hannah was Persephone, she had the unique ability to make plants grow," Zel said, with a slight shake of her head. "You should have seen what she did to the palace in Hell."

"How are you getting these powers?" Belial asked. "First darkness, now this. You never had them in your other lives."

"I believe it's my Archangel gift, allowing me to tap into

the powers from my past lives," I said, as I caused more plants to grow around us. Even when I'd believed I was human, I'd sought out plants and flowers, finding them soothing and restorative. I'd been unable to unlock this power until I felt Faerie's energy all around me, but it had been inside me all along—a reminder of my life as Persephone. My fae powers from the Spring Court were back too, allowing me to control air as well.

Kassiel nodded like he could follow my thoughts. "Yes, that makes sense. Jophiel's power made people forget. Your power is to remember."

My smile fell at the mention of my sister, but it did make a strange sort of sense. I'd recovered most of my memories from my previous lives, and now I was able to tap into those powers too. "Let's hope I can help Lucifer do the same."

Everyone had come through the portal now, with Mirabella stepping through last. The portal closed behind her and the gem in her hand dulled. "The High King lives in the castle at the top of that hill," she said, pointing ahead of us at a large mountain with a gleaming white fairy tale castle on top of it, with spires and arches and silver towers. "This is where messengers and other visitors wait to be granted entrance. Transport should arrive shortly."

"We could always just fly up there," Belial muttered.

"It's best to follow the High King's protocols," Mirabella said. "Those who cross him don't often survive."

"I met him once, and I have to agree," Kassiel added, his mouth twisting.

Zel rested her hands on her daggers. "Something's coming."

Shapes appeared on the horizon, and I shielded my eyes with my hand as I watched them approach. "What are they?"

"Griffins," Mirabella said. "From the High King's personal fleet. It's a great honor."

The beasts touched down in the courtyard, surprisingly light on their taloned feet and graceful for such large creatures. They had the bodies of lions and the wings and heads of eagles, and on their backs they had golden saddles with fae riders sitting in them. There was no mistaking the riders as anything other than fae, with their pointed ears, ethereal beauty, and unusually colored hair.

Most surprising of all—my son Damien rode at the front of them.

As he dismounted his griffin, I rushed toward him, unable to help myself. Of all my sons, Damien was the one who most resembled me—or at the least me when I had been Persephone. His eyes were the color of periwinkles and his hair was an indigo so dark it looked black until the light hit it and revealed the truth of his fae heritage. As a prince of the Spring Court, he wore a small crown of gold with jeweled flowers, along with a billowy black silk shirt and trousers, plain but obviously made by the finest tailors. He flashed me a charming smile as I approached, the one that had always made me forgive him no matter what he'd done—and he'd always been a very mischievous child.

"Damien!" I drew him close, my heart overflowing with

love. It had been so many decades since I'd seen him last, in another life entirely. "Or should I call you Dionysus?"

He made a pained face and laughed. "No, I don't use that name any longer. Damien is fine."

I pulled back to really look at him, noticing a darkness in his gaze that had never been there before, though his smile never faltered. "I missed you so much."

"It's always too long between your lives. Though I heard Father put an end to the curse finally. Kassiel's told me a few things, but I'd love to hear about it from you."

I reached up to touch his glorious hair, so beautiful under the sun. "Yes, we have lots to catch up on."

"Indeed." He grinned and swatted my hand away from his hair. "Like how you're carrying my sister."

"It's weird, isn't it?" Kassiel asked, as he drew closer to us. "We've all lived for hundreds of years, yet now we're getting a baby sister."

"Not so weird to us," Belial said. "We went through it with you, after all."

"It's good to see you both again," Damien said, and the brothers all did those manly hugs that mostly consisted of back-patting and grunting. My heart melted at the sight of the three of them together for the first time in...well, probably centuries. Our family was finally reunited once again. The only person missing was Lucifer. I resolved once more to get him back, and to recreate this moment again with him at my side.

"Good to see *me*, you mean." Kassiel lifted his chin at Belial with a grin. "We're still not sure about this guy."

Damien arched an eyebrow. "What's he done now?"

"I'll tell you later," Kassiel said, while Belial scowled at them both.

"I look forward to the full report." Damien gestured toward the castle above us. "Right now the High King is waiting, and I suggest we make haste."

"Yes, we don't want to keep him waiting," I said. "Especially since I have a feeling we'll need his help."

"Then let's begin the next part of your journey." Damien stepped forward, placing his hand on my elbow. He led me toward the griffins, and the other fae riders stood and bowed their heads. We stopped in front of one that had been tethered to Damien's griffin and had no rider.

"I haven't seen griffins in so long." I reached out and allowed the griffin to nudge its head against my fingertips. Its warm breath fanned over my skin and its curved beak poked against my hand. Without warning, it dropped to its knees, turning its head inquisitively as it seemed to wait for my next move.

"She's accepted you," Damien said with a smile. "That's an invitation to climb on her back."

I ran my fingers through her luxurious white feathers as I settled onto soft, golden fur and a firm saddle. Like most magical beings of myth and legend, griffins were native to Faerie, and they served as transportation for the nobles of the different courts. "It's good to know I haven't lost my touch with magical beings after all these years."

Damien mounted the griffin beside me. "I never had any doubts."

My companions were seated behind the fae riders, and I was the only one honored with a griffin of my own. I hoped I remembered how to ride one.

Once everyone was settled on their griffins, our beasts leaped into the air and spread their wings, taking us toward the castle and one of the most dangerous men alive—the High King of the Fae.

8.

HANNAH

We flew through the air toward Oberon's castle, and riding the griffin was entirely different from flying under the power of my own wings, with her sleek muscles flexing beneath my thighs and the steady beat of her wings sending currents of air to wash over me.

The castle loomed before us, sparkling in the sunlight as if the entire building was made of crystal. Perhaps it was. Turrets stretched high into the air, with colorful flags representing each of the different courts waving slowly against the blue sky. Even here there were trees and flowers everywhere, seamlessly woven into the architecture. The fae were deeply in tune with nature and the elements, one of the few things I missed about being one of them.

The griffins set down in the courtyard in front of the palace, where dozens of guards in elaborate silver armor and plumed helmets were stationed. A man in fine livery stood on the wide steps leading up to the massive door inlaid with gems and carved with ancient runes. He bowed low as I approached, with my guards and companions fanning out behind me, and my sons at my side.

"Your majesty, the High King is expecting you," he said. "Please follow me."

The man cast a slightly disparaging glance over my group as the door opened behind him, moving silently despite its size. He led us inside the palace, into a great entry filled with more guards and a few noble fae dressed in their finest clothes with hair in every shade of the rainbow. I looked closely, but didn't recognize any of them. Not really a surprise, since it had been many centuries since I'd been Persephone, and I'd spent much of my time in Hell during that life anyway.

As the man led us further into the castle, I took in my surroundings and felt like I'd gone back in time—or stepped into my previous life. Almost nothing had changed in hundreds of years in this castle, and I suspected that was true of all of Faerie. Technology didn't work in this realm, and the fae were resistant to change in general. It was one reason they preferred to stay neutral in conflicts and to live in isolation here in Faerie, with very few people coming or going from this realm.

An air of hushed calm hung in each of the spaces we moved through, until we stopped in a waiting room outside two large doors that I remembered led to the throne room. There were other fae here chatting with each other, all nobles judging by their clothes and the jewels decorating their bodies. Each one was dressed in elegant clothes that looked like something from the 1800s, and they gave us judgmental looks as we entered. My group was all dressed for combat, not courtly life, but there was nothing to be done about that now.

A tall, willowy woman stood by the window, and she wore a pastel pink gown of the finest silk. Her hair was the color of purple hydrangea and atop it was a crown similar to Damien's, but much more elaborate. She turned slowly, revealing herself in such a way that my breath froze in my chest.

"Mother?" I stepped forward to greet her, but her periwinkle blue eyes were cool and devoid of care as she leveled her gaze at me. Demeter was the Queen of the Spring Court and my mother when I'd been Persephone. It had been many centuries since I'd seen her, and my heart overflowed with joy at the thought of reconnecting with another member of my family.

She took me in slowly, her eyes scanning me head to toe while a tight frown crossed her lips. "You're not my daughter in this life."

I drew back as if she'd slapped me across the face. How could she be so callous and cruel? My children were no less mine because this wasn't the body that had birthed them, and she would always be my mother, no matter how long it had been.

"Mother, please." I hated explaining myself, and tried not to sound weak as I asked for the recognition of our relationship. "I know I've been gone for a long time, but I've regained my memories and my powers. I am truly your daughter once more. In mind and spirit, if not in body."

"I mourned my daughter's death. She is gone, and you...you are a stranger." She walked past my group, leaving the fragrance of lavender in her wake. Her words cut deep into me, and I stared after her as she joined another group of fae with her back to me.

Even Damien looked shocked and horrified by his grandmother's comments. "I'm sorry. I asked her to come with me to this meeting, but I didn't realize she would react that way upon seeing you."

"It's not your fault." I sighed, and tried now to show how much it bothered me. Demeter had always been a difficult mother, and some things never changed. After all, she'd made Lucifer agree to that ridiculous deal that had forced me to spend half my time in Hell and half my time here in Faerie, even though I'd been a grown adult who could make my own decisions about my life. To call her an overbearing parent was putting it lightly.

All thoughts of my mother vanished when the man who'd led us here held up a thin, silver fanfare trumpet, which he began to blow as soon the doors opened to admit us. I stepped inside the throne room first, walking down a long white carpet with my entourage behind me. In here there were even more guards in full armor, along with more nobles in long gowns or elegant suits who studied us with haughty looks.

The man we'd followed in bowed deeply from the waist.

"Presenting Queen Hannah of the demons, along with her guests."

High King Oberon sat on a wide stage on a huge throne of tooled gold and silver designed by some of the finest craftsmen in Faerie. Exquisite metal vines twisted together so that it looked like the king was sitting on a chair made of plants and flowers, yet he managed to lounge as if he was completely relaxed. Behind him were huge windows looking out at the sky, with a stunning view of much of Faerie below it.

The most powerful fae of all time focused his eyes on me, while my group bowed low to him. I nearly bowed too, and then remembered that I was his equal now. Above his pointed ears was a crown done in the same style as his throne, and he had long black hair and cold eyes, with an expression that somehow looked both bored and cruel all at once.

"It's been a long time," he said to me in his haughty voice. "I preferred you as Persephone, though I do enjoy the irony of you being an angel now. And Demon Queen, no less."

It took all my self-control not to roll my eyes. Was everyone in this realm stuck on the idea of me as Persephone? Yet while I might have changed, Oberon was still the same asshole as always.

Though I did notice one change from my previous life—there was no throne beside him anymore. I'd recently learned that my aunt, his wife, Titania, was dead, and most believed that Oberon was responsible. She was my mother's older sister and a powerful fae queen, but she'd been unable to produce children, and in Oberon's desperation to have a son and heir, he had many affairs. In retaliation, she cursed him to only have daughters. The rumor was that for many years he'd tried everything to break the curse, but when nothing worked, he'd killed Titania in a fit of rage. I believed it. The man was evil. Unfortunately, I had to play nice while in his realm.

I gritted my teeth behind my tight, closed-lipped smile. "Thank you for seeing us on such short notice. As you saw in my message, Lucifer has recently escaped the confines of Heaven."

"You mean War," Oberon corrected. "I suspect there is little left of Lucifer in there."

"We'll see about that." My fingernails bit into my palms as I forced myself to keep my cool. "He wants to start a war that will encompass all the realms, including Faerie. He must be stopped—and we believe the only way to do so is to use another Elder God."

A few shocked gasps went up around the throne room before it fell into deathly silence once more. Oberon straightened at my words and curved his hands over the arms of his throne. "You wish to release Famine."

"We do, yes."

He tilted his head as he considered. "Releasing one Horseman to stop another is a risky gamble. Still, Famine hates War, so you may have some success if you wish them to battle it out. But then what do you do with the winner? Or the loser, for that matter?" He stroked his chin. "There might be another way to save Lucifer."

"What is it?" I asked, unable to hide my eagerness. I'd searched all the books for any other solution, but hadn't come across anything viable, but perhaps Oberon had knowledge even more ancient than I could access.

"If someone is possessed by an Elder God, that person can wage the battle inside themselves—an internal fight to defeat the god and take their powers." He raised his eyebrows. "Only a few people would be strong enough to do such a thing, but Lucifer is one of them."

My heart sank. "Except he failed."

Belial turned to me. "He only failed because he lost all his memories of you, so he didn't want to fight War. He has no reason to wish for peace without you."

"He's right," Damien said. "You were always the one to calm Father, from the very beginning."

Kassiel nodded. "And it's because of you that he ended the war with the angels at all."

A tiny ray of hope fluttered in my chest again. "So if we could get his memories back, he might be able to fight War and defeat him. But he sacrificed those memories—how would we get them back?"

No one seemed to have an answer for that.

Oberon waved a lazy hand. "Perhaps it's impossible. You may have to trap the Horsemen again in tombs, as we did in the old times. Or you could always try to send them to Void."

Void—the realm where all the Elder Gods lived. It was completely sealed off from anyone entering or escaping it, mainly to protect all the other realms from the powerful beings inside it.

"How would we do that?" I asked.

"Lucifer had a key to Void long ago," Oberon said. "Given to him by his father. Perhaps he still has it hidden away somewhere?"

"I don't remember anything about the location of a key." I turned to the others who'd come with me. "Do any of you?"

All of them murmured no or shook their heads. Damn. Another dead end. Even if I wanted to send Lucifer to Void, which I would only do as a last resort, the places he might have concealed a key were too numerous to count. It would take far longer to search for it than it would take Pestilence and War to destroy the realms between them.

I drew in a breath as the path ahead became clear. "Then we have no choice but to release Famine."

"Do you have someone willing to make the sacrifice?" Oberon asked.

Azazel stepped forward. "I'll do it."

"I also volunteer," Belial said.

"As do I," Damien chimed in.

Oberon drummed his fingers on the throne. "Perhaps one of you is strong enough to control Famine. Perhaps not. I'll be sending some of my own people with you to be certain it's handled correctly."

"I wouldn't expect anything less." In truth, I'd worried he might come with us. After all, he was one of the people who had trapped the Four Horsemen originally, and I thought he might want to be there when the one in his realm was released. I supposed Oberon didn't like getting his hands dirty anymore. He'd been different back when I was Eve. Not such an asshole. A real leader to his people.

The High King raised his chin. "I can't have a Horseman of the Apocalypse traipsing about my realm. We've kept Famine contained so long due to our strong ties with nature, but once that tomb is open, there's no telling what will happen to our realm."

"You know I will not allow Famine to harm Faerie," Damien said, with a small bow to his uncle. "If I must be the one to make the sacrifice, I would do it to protect our people."

"I know you would. That's the only reason I'm allowing this endeavor at all." Oberon's eyes hardened and his voice turned sharp. "And if all else fails—make sure to open a portal to Earth so Famine can destroy that world instead of ours."

Yep. Still an asshole.

9

LUCIFER

Las Vegas was sprawled out below me, all the lights, all the power, all the greed. I breathed it in, using it like fuel before turning my attention to The Celestial and my penthouse at the top. It wouldn't take me long to amass my demon warriors and lead them forth into battle. As soon as the angels arrived, we'd wreak havoc and destruction upon them, and on the unsuspecting mortals residing in the area. None would be spared my wrath.

My wings beat against the night as I soared over the city, concealed by darkness. Something about flying by the Stratosphere tickled my mind, like a memory I couldn't retrieve, but then War's presence crushed the feeling. He was always there, entwined with my own self, and soon I forgot anything except overwhelming rage.

I dropped down in front of The Celestial, sheathed my wings, and adjusted my suit. This time I planned to enter my kingdom properly, and I would announce myself to my people so they knew who they truly served. As for the woman? I planned to lock her away, keeping her caged like a songbird until she gave birth to my child. Then I would decide what to do with her.

But as I stepped inside my casino I noticed it was disturbingly empty, and heard shouts and screams up ahead by the bar. I walked quickly, passing human bodies on the ground around the blackjack tables and in front of the slot machines, each one an unnatural color and covered in putrid boils. A few were still alive, groaning and clutching their heads or chests, their features set in grim masks as they writhed on the carpet.

Pestilence. The name slithered through me, my whole body reacting to the slimy feel of it. Yes, he was here. Another Horseman. A brother of sorts, though not one welcome at my door. But why was he here? What did he seek? Did he plan to ally with me—or challenge me?

I found him at the Styx Bar, surrounded by gargoyles in stone form, who were managing to hold him off and resist his attacks, though I suspected that wouldn't last for long. They paused when they saw me, some of them opening their mouths in shock and fear, though some turned hopeful eyes upon me, as if I might save them from their fate. Save them I would, but only because they belonged to me. I wrapped my power around them, bending them to my will, taking away all their thoughts except those of combat and violence.

Pestilence turned toward me and snarled, his eyes glowing white and filled with madness. The body he'd claimed had not fared well under his control, and his skin was yellow and blistered, his hair white and thin, and his body reeked of decay and disease. Just being this close to him made me feel contaminated, though my powers protected me from much of his sickness.

"Why are you here?" I asked in a way that stiffened Pestilence's shoulders. "This is my domain."

"You know why." He cocked his head with a manic grin. "Or perhaps you don't. Have you forgotten our ancient feud as well?"

His words stirred something inside me, but once again it was just out of reach. The body he'd taken had belonged to Gadreel, a Fallen who had once served me, who turned out to be the reincarnation of Adam. I remembered all of that, though not why he'd betrayed me, nor why I carried such immense hatred for Adam.

I clenched my hands into fists and allowed my anger to seep out of me in a red glow. "What do you want? Answer me!"

His own putrid yellow power emanated from him too, clashing against my own. "I'm here for Eve."

"Eve?" I knew no one by that name.

He let out a sharp laugh. "You really don't remember. Good. That will make this much easier. Step aside and I'll get her out of your hair so you can continue with your plans of war. You can have this place. All I want is Eve."

My eyes narrowed as his words stirred up a fresh wave of wrath inside me, and my heart beat like Strife's hooves were thundering over my ribs. "You speak of the woman living in my penthouse."

Pestilence stepped forward with a challenge in his eyes. "She belongs to me, and I'm here to claim her."

"No." The worst burst out of me so vehemently it made the liquor bottles and the mirrors in the bar shake. It even made Pestilence step back, toward the gargoyle warriors under my control, who patiently waited to unleash their frenzy, though they snapped their teeth at him and tried to scratch him with their talons.

Pestilence lifted an eyebrow. "Are we back to this age-old fight then?"

I didn't know what he was saying, but I knew, deep in my bones, down in my very soul, that the woman—Hannah or Eve or whatever she was called—wasn't his. The life inside her wasn't his. They were *mine*. All mine.

"Get out of my hotel." I spat the words.

"It doesn't need to be like this," he said. "Not anymore. We're the same now. Two Horsemen of the Apocalypse, with the same goals of spreading chaos upon the land. We can forget the past—hell, you've already done that—and move forward as brothers. Once we release Famine and Death we'll be even stronger. We'll rule all the realms—even Void itself."

I stepped closer to him, forcing him back against the wall, my hands balled into fists. "I'm already the king here, and I'm not good at sharing. Get the fuck out of here before I destroy you."

He met my gaze, one corner of his lips lifting. "You can try, but you both know we can't be killed."

"Pestilence can't—but that body can."

I brought one of my fists up and landed it on his face, bursting one of the throbbing pustules there. The fluid inside it burned like acid as it ran over my skin, but I shook it off. I wasn't done. I summoned my sword and prepared to strike him down, but he slithered away like the slippery beast he was.

When I turned to face him, he stood on the other side of the bar wielding a bow and arrows. Each tip pulsed with yellow and black power, a combination of his Pestilence sickness and his Fallen darkness. He unleashed arrows faster than humanly possible, but I threw up a shield of darkness to stop him, then blasted him with blue hellfire laced with red rage. He launched over it with sickly gray wings that had lost a lot of feathers, and he was surprisingly spry for someone who looked so ill. I released my gargoyle guards and they leaped in front of him, blocking his path. He turned back to me and fired off more arrows, but he wasn't fast enough against me, a being created for one purpose: to fight.

I launched myself forward and sliced into him with my sword. He let out a horrifying screech, then managed to stab me with one of his arrows. Weakness and disease coursed through me, trying to slow me down, but I struggled against his powers, refusing to let him stop me. I couldn't let him get to that woman or my child. I'd burn this whole place down before I let that happen.

I lifted the sword and slashed at him, cutting into his shoulder and down his chest. He let out a horrifying screech as the hellfire stung him, and then he barreled through the gargoyles as he flew out of the casino. I rushed after him, my own wings giving me speed, but once I made it outside I saw him jump on his horse and ride away, slipping into the crowd of tourists and gamblers. Screams followed in his wake, but his horse was so fast, many had barely any time to react as he passed by them.

"Follow him," I commanded my gargoyles. They weren't as fast as his horse was, but since he was injured, they might have a chance of catching up. I could have gone after him, but I had more pressing business here, and I was satisfied that the fucker wouldn't return to challenge me anytime soon.

Besides, I had to check on the woman before I did anything else. Though I felt only hatred and rage toward her, I needed to be sure my child was protected.

I flew up to the penthouse, but it was dark. There was no one inside.

The woman was gone.

10

HANNAH

Huge white columns soared into the air, gleaming under the soft moonlight at the temple where Famine's tomb was located. Our griffins circled over it, allowing us to take in the entire structure. It clearly hadn't been touched in many years, and nature had nearly swallowed it up entirely. All except for the massive statue of Oberon at the front of it. It had to be at least forty feet tall and depicted him seated on a throne decorated with gold and precious stones, while wearing a crown and holding a scepter in one hand. The entrance to the temple was underneath the throne, so you had to pass under Oberon's watchful eyes to enter.

There had once been a similar statue on Earth in Greece, depicting Oberon in his guise as Zeus. For many years he'd been worshiped on Earth under that name, but the statue had been destroyed long ago. Only its counterpart here in Faerie remained.

The day had passed from the awakening of spring, though the heat of midsummer, and now we were relaxing in a temperate fall that was rapidly cooling to winter. The light had changed, growing softer, falling in pale strips between the columns as our griffins sat down in front of the statue. I dismounted, taking in the untouched surroundings. I hadn't been here since I was Eve, when we first sealed Famine away. Belial had only been a child then. There was nothing else for miles except for this temple and the thick, dark forest surrounding it.

"Of course the entrance to the tomb would be under his feet," Belial muttered, as we took in the stone doors in front of us. They were covered in vines and other plants that had grown wild, but I flicked a hand and they released their hold on the stone and retreated back into the earth.

Damien cast his eyes up at the statue with distaste. "Yes. Oberon would trust no one else to guard a thing as dangerous as Famine."

I turned back to take in the large group of people who had come with me on this mission. My sons, all three of them eager and determined to save their father, despite any issues they had with him. My nephew Callan, hovering near me protectively, and Azazel, who stood with a grim set to her mouth. Theo was organizing his gargoyle guards into a formation around the tomb, while the fae warriors sent by High King Oberon stood impassively to the side, as if they could only be bothered to get involved should something go wrong. Our messenger Mirabella, who I'd learned had a father in the Autumn Court, stood apart from them, ready to open a portal for us back to Earth whenever we wished.

"We're all ready," Kassiel said. "The fae are opening the temple doors now."

I nodded, before turning to Zel. "Do you still want to do this?"

She scowled. "Want to? Not exactly. But it needs to be done, and I'm the best person for the job."

I took her face in my hands and stared into her dark eyes. "Promise me you'll fight Famine and will somehow remain yourself. I can't lose you too, Zel."

She put her hands over mine and gazed back at me with determination and love. "I promise. Long ago I swore to protect you and to fight by your side, and I'm not stopping now."

I nodded and stepped back, blinking away tears in my eyes. "I love you."

"Don't get all mushy on me, little angel," Zel said with a grin, her face softening. Then she brought me in for a tight squeeze and whispered, "I love you too, but don't you dare tell anyone."

The temple door opened with a loud rumble and a plume of dust, and Zel and I stepped back to watch. I couldn't see anything inside except darkness, but Callan and I could fix that with some angelic light.

"Let's move," I told my team, gesturing toward the entrance. So far there was no sign of Nemesis or Fenrir, but I didn't want to stick around and wait for them to show up either.

Theo went in first with some of his guards, along with Callan, who lit the way with a bright ball of hovering light. I went in next with Azazel, Damien, and Kassiel, using my own light to illuminate a dusty stone corridor with stale air, barely large enough for two of us to pass through side by side. More of my gargoyle guards trailed behind me, along with a few fae warriors at the back. The rest stayed outside, in case any threat should arise there.

The hallway became more of a tunnel, slanting down, down, down. No one had been inside this temple in thousands of years, and as we went deeper into the Earth, the space became more and more oppressive. I couldn't wait to get back outside.

Eventually the downward slope of the tunnel led us to another large door, this one covered in magical runes just like Pestilence's and War's tombs had been. The air here was especially stifling, and my stomach turned at the horrible power emanating from within the tomb. The baby kicked too, and I rested my hand over her, trying to silently reassure her.

"This is it," Callan said. "Famine's tomb."

Kassiel examined it closely. "It's built right into the temple itself."

Belial gestured at Damien to go forward. "You're up. Make us proud."

Damien grimaced, but stepped close to the door and pulled out a small knife. Only a few people could open Famine's tomb, including Oberon himself, or one of his daughters—and my son Damien. To do so, you had to be born in this realm, with the blood of one of the people who had sealed the tomb originally.

Damien looked over at me and I nodded, though inside I was trembling. We had to do this, but that didn't mean I was ready for what was about to happen. Were we really going to release the third Horseman upon the world? Would this plan work, or were we only bring doom upon ourselves?

Damien drew the blade across his palm in a neat slice. I winced, but he didn't so much as flinch, and then he pressed his bloody hand against the tomb's door. The runes began to glow, casting all of us in an eerie green haze. Then the door flew open with a burst of power so strong it knocked all of us back. I slammed against the nearest wall, and only my newly-remembered air magic cushioned my blow and protected the baby.

"I'm free," a horrible, croaking voice sounded from inside the dark depths of the tomb, and then a cloud of sickly green seeped out of the tomb with the smell of decaying plants and rotten food. As we all recovered from the blast and got back on our feet, the green fog coalesced into the vague shape of a woman, though her features were blurred and kept shifting like smoke. "I am Famine...and I must feed. Who will make the sacrifice and gain my powers?"

"The third Horseman is a woman?" Callan asked beside me.

Zel rose to her feet and dusted herself off. "I will make the sacrifice."

As soon as the words had left her mouth, one of the fae guards moved behind her and stabbed a sword through her chest. I screamed as Zel was impaled, then saw through the fae guard's magical disguise—revealing a gorgeous woman with fiery red hair. Nemesis.

I blasted her back with a gust of air, while Callan jumped forward to catch Zel as she fell. Blood gushed from her chest, and I cursed myself for not allowing Marcus to come with us, and for not seeing through Nemesis's illusions sooner. I'd barely paid the fae guards who'd followed us inside any attention, and now Zel was dying. What could I do?

"Take her body and heal her," I yelled at Famine, as I desperately tried to cover Zel's wounds and stop the bleeding. Zel was barely conscious, her body shutting down as it tried to heal itself.

"No," the rasping, feminine voice boomed. "She is too weak. She would not survive."

Two gargoyle guards I recognized suddenly rushed into the area, and one of them yelled, "My queen, shifters attack outside the temple! We're surrounded!"

I swore under my breath, and turned to the others with me. "Defend the perimeter and get Zel to a healer! I can stop Nemesis myself." When my sons all looked like they would argue with me, I held up a hand and yelled, "Go!"

Callan carried Zel outside, and I prayed it wasn't the last time I would see her alive. Damien and Kassiel followed, along with some of the guards, though Theo and Belial stayed with me.

Famine's form began moving toward the exit too. "I hunger...who will feed me?"

"I will," Belial said, moving in front of Famine, shielding the rest of us with his body. My heart lurched into my throat at the thought of my son becoming a Horseman—but he was also probably the best option here, I was sad to admit.

Famine sneered at him, and then with one ghostly hand she knocked him aside. "I require a female host."

"Take me," Nemesis rose to her feet, with her imps—who had all been disguised as fae guards—behind her wielding weapons. "I'm the one you want."

Famine's green spectral form moved toward her, but there was no way in Heaven or Hell I was letting Nemesis get control of this Elder God. This was my one chance to rescue Lucifer from War, and I wasn't going to lose it. Nemesis had betrayed us time and time again, and now she'd stabbed Zel—I wasn't letting her win.

"No." I strode forward with both darkness and light emanating from me, my air powers whipping at my hair, while thorny vines grew up out of the ground at my feet. It was time to show that bitch what happened when you crossed the Demon Queen. "Famine is mine."

My thick vines wrapped around Nemesis, stabbing into her bare skin with the thorns, but she grew long, black talons and sliced through them, then managed to scamper away to the other side of the cave. Belial and Theo began fighting against the other imps, but the only one that mattered to me was Nemesis.

She split herself into dozens of copies, all of them slashing at me with swords and claws, but I cast out the light of truth around me and found the real Nemesis. I shot her with light and darkness, but she was so fast she seemed to almost blink away, and managed to dodge everything. No way was she escaping though. With a roar, I created a tornado of air laced with light and darkness, then unleashed it upon her. It caught Nemesis inside it, and then my vines reached up and tore her apart, limb from bloody limb. Though I'd never reveled in death, I watched on with grim satisfaction as Nemesis was destroyed.

Don't fuck with a pregnant woman protecting her family.

"My queen, are you all right?" Theo limped to my side, one hand wrapped around his waist.

Imp corpses were scattered over the ground, and Belial delivered the final blow to one of them with Morningstar. Then he turned to survey the pieces of Nemesis lying all over the ground in a pool of blood.

"Shit, Mother," Belial said. "I never realized you were so brutal."

"I did what I had to do." I looked around the cave and my breath caught. "Where is Famine?"

Belial sheathed his sword. "She must have escaped during the battle."

We rushed up the tunnel and emerged into a snowy battlefield. Shifters and imps fought against gargoyles and fae, and I was relieved to see that both Damien and Kassiel were all right. I scanned the area and found Famine's green spectral form floating above them all. She hovered over Mirabella for a few seconds, then turned around and reached for a large white wolf with ice coating its fur, who stood beside Fenrir.

Famine was looking for a new host. I couldn't let that happen. But Zel was gone, carried off by Callan to safety, and Famine wanted a female body.

There was only one person strong to contain her.

Me.

11

HANNAH

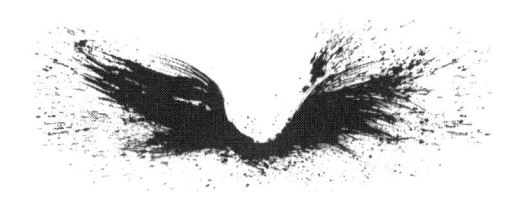

A path of dead, brown vegetation led directly to Famine. Plants withered and died, flowers lost their petals, leaves turned black. Shifters and gargoyles alike fell to their knees in her path, as if they'd lost all the strength to fight or even stand.

She was feeding.

Everything about it made my soul revolt. I was a goddess of spring and nature, and she was the opposite of everything I held dear. Yet I had to offer myself to her...there was no other choice.

Fenrir, in his giant wolf form, saw Famine coming for the ice wolf and jumped in front of her, baring his fangs. Whoever that wolf was, Fenrir didn't want her taken over by Famine. And here I'd thought Fenrir didn't care about anything or anyone except himself. But Famine couldn't be stopped, not by Fenrir, and she tossed him aside, then closed in on the white wolf.

I unfurled my silver wings and launched myself toward Famine, using my wind powers to give me a boost. "Famine!" I yelled.

The Elder God turned toward me, just as the ice wolf shifted back into a beautiful woman with white hair and pointed ears. She pulled out a gem and activated it, using a key to open a portal that she and Fenrir slipped inside. It closed before Famine could escape back to Earth. Like the coward he was, Fenrir had turned tail again—and left behind most of his shifters.

Famine let out a frustrated growl now that her host had vanished, but then her energy turned upon me. Being near her was like facing an energy drain—her very presence made me feel tired, hungry, and weak. Like I hadn't eaten or slept in days.

"I command you to submit," I said, repeating words I'd heard Belial use with Pestilence, but then I added my own twist. "Famine, I need your help."

"Is that so?" she asked with a sickening cackle.

"I need to defeat War. I'm told you are the only one who can stop him."

Her spectral form grew dark and angry. "Yes...War must suffer..."

Not exactly what I wanted, but I let it slide. "Serve me, and we'll take him down together."

"Mother, no!" Belial called out. He stood beside Kassiel and Damien, who also echoed his sentiments, but I ignored them. My sons had to know this was the only way now that Famine was freed.

"Are you willing to make the sacrifice?" Famine asked.

I hesitated. I was willing to do anything to save Lucifer...except endanger our unborn child. "That depends on what you ask of me. I am with child, and I won't let you do anything that would hurt her."

Famine's essence moved closer as she considered me. The entire glade around the temple fell silent as everyone watched our exchange. No one fought anymore—they were too weak thanks to Famine anyway.

"I was a mother once too," she said in a quieter voice. "Perhaps you know my son, Baal."

"I do, yes. He is an ally of mine." I vaguely remembered Baal saying that Famine was his parent, but I'd stupidly assumed he meant his father.

"There were other children too," Famine continued. "War murdered some of them. The others...perhaps they are still alive. Perhaps I will be able to find them."

"Then you understand that I would do anything to protect my child."

"Yes. I will not hurt this child. I swear it."

Relief loosened my chest around the breath I'd been holding. As an Elder God, she couldn't lie. "Then what sacrifice would you ask of me?"

"The sacrifice of your fertility. Your baby will remain safe and whole. She will be powerful and strong. I will ensure it. But this child will be your last. After she is born, your body will bring forth life no more."

I wrapped my arms around myself as her words sank in. The last. It was difficult to contemplate. I hadn't given thought to having more babies after this one, but the idea that it would be impossible made me feel hollow inside. I smoothed my hand over my bump, feeling the baby move inside, knowing once she was born I'd never experience this miracle again.

I swallowed hard as tears pricked my eyes, but then I turned and looked at my three smart, brave, handsome sons. Lucifer and I had been blessed with them and with this daughter growing inside me now. As long as this unborn child would be safe, I could accept never having another one after her.

"I accept this sacrifice."

"Very good." Famine moved toward me in a way that reminded me of a swarm of bees. "I'm looking forward to being a mother again."

Something in the way she spoke the words iced my blood. There was a finality in her tone, as though the child would be hers, and not mine. She thought she would take control of me, but I was going to fight. I remembered Oberon's words about how one could defeat and then become an Elder God, just as Famine's ghostly form surrounded me. Her power enveloped me and seeped into my skin, oozing into my pores, sliding into every hole until she'd slithered deep into my soul. Overwhelming hunger and desperate need made me nearly tear out my eyes, along with a melancholy so strong I could barely breathe. I was fueled by deep, intense longing, not just for food, but for power. For life.

Fighting against Famine's immense power was impossible. How had I ever thought I'd be able to defeat her? She stretched through my body, taking it over, claiming me as her host, and I couldn't stop her. No wonder Lucifer hadn't found his way without his memories. He'd never had a chance.

I gazed across the battlefield, at the dead grass and the weakened beings all kneeling before me. I could see their auras, their power, their essence, and I breathed it in, drawing upon their strength, claiming it as mine. It was my nature to feed, and none could stop me from draining every last living thing around me. Only then would I be strong enough to stop War.

My eyes fell upon the three men before me, the ones who called my name over and over. Damien sagged, his beautiful skin dimming as I sucked away his life force. Kassiel was on his hands and knees, his face pale. Belial, the oldest and strongest, fought back the hardest, but even he eventually fell under my might.

As he hit the ground, my senses came back to me and I recoiled. What was I doing? I couldn't allow Famine to leech power from those I loved. Those were my children she was draining, and behind them, my friends and my allies. I had to stop her from killing them all. I had to gain control somehow.

I forced myself to release the energy I'd stolen, allowing it to return to the people around me. Famine tried to exert control over me again, but this time, I knew what she was doing and I fought back. I could feel it now, a duality where I needed to hold on to myself, to make myself strong so that I didn't fade behind Famine. She would be the driving force if I let her, until we merged into one terrible, awful being that would drain the life out of every living thing in every realm, until there was nothing left.

Famine struggled harder, pouring more of her power over me, while attempting to reach out and steal life from everything around us. I countered her by sending out living energy into the surroundings with my Persephone powers, bringing the plants back to life around us, fighting her blight with my power of growth. That only made her more angry, but it also made me realize something—I was the direct counter of Famine. She made crops wither and die, and I made them grow and flourish.

I was Persephone, the goddess of spring and death. I was Eve, who had trapped the Four Horsemen originally. And I was Hannah, an angel of truth, and the motherfucking Demon Queen. Famine thought she could take over my body and raise my child as her own, but she had no idea how powerful I was. Especially because it wasn't just me. I had my daughter too, a little piece of Lucifer nestled in my body. My baby was strong, and together I knew we could subdue Famine and contain her.

My daughter kicked like she understood my need for us to fight together, and I drew on my love for Lucifer to center myself. I gazed upon my sons, all of them standing again and looking at me with such love it overwhelmed me. My family was my strength. Love gave me power.

This is my body, I told Famine. *And you will submit to me.*

Never, she cried, as she raged inside me. The overwhelming feeling of desperation, need, and hunger that could never be sated filled me, but I stared at my sons and pushed it down. I focused on life and love, using my memories of all my past lives to fuel me. I'd been reborn hundreds of times, my soul strengthening every time, and each life had given me a tiny bit more power. Enough power to defeat even an Elder God.

I forced Famine into a small space inside me, squeezing her tighter and tighter, draining her of strength and will until she faded away into nothing. The intense hunger and longing vanished, along with her presence. The only thing that remained was her power, coursing through my body like crackling electricity, now mine to control.

Famine was gone, and I remained.

No, that wasn't right.

I was Famine now.

An Elder God. A Horseman of the Apocalypse. A being powerful enough to stop War.

A black horse appeared out of the night and rode toward me, and I held out my hand to her nose. She breathed over me with warmth and recognition as she nudged against my fingers. I knew this horse, and it knew me. *Misery*, something inside me supplied. That was her name.

As I pondered this strange bond with this horse I'd just met, my sons rushed over to me. "What was that?" Belial's knuckles were white around the hilt of Morningstar, which was glowing with both white and black light.

"Are you okay?" Kassiel asked.

Damien peered at me. "Is Famine in there?"

"I *am* Famine." I stroked the horse's flank, then turned to face them with wonder. "But I'm also still me."

Belial arched an eyebrow. "You defeated her?"

Kassiel grinned. "Of course she did."

"How?" Damien asked.

"I used my love for my family to give me strength," I said, rubbing my bump as I smiled at my sons.

"That's corny as fuck," Belial said, rolling his eyes.

"Maybe, but it worked, didn't it?" I gave each of them a warm hug, so relieved to still be myself, but now with added hope. If I could defeat Famine, then surely Lucifer could defeat War too. He just needed me to guide him and help him remember who he was.

I glanced around the area, and most of the shifters and imps had either fled or been killed. Most of my people were still standing, except for Callan and Zel. They were on the ground under a dead tree, and I rushed over to them.

"How is she?" I asked.

Callan looked up at me with a pained expression. "She needs a healer right away."

While Damien called for Mirabella to open the portal to Earth, I kneeled beside my best friend and placed my hand on her cheek. She was weak, and I felt her life force in a way I never had before. A little voice told me it would be so easy to drain her of what was left—the lingering remnant of Famine's essence, perhaps. Something I would have to learn to live with and control.

But if I could take energy and life, could I give it too? I was able to do it with plants, why not people?

I rested my hands over the huge, bloody gash in Zel's stomach, which I'd avoided looking at because it was too horrifying to consider. While angelic healers like Marcus used their connection to the light to heal, I was different, and my power came from nature. Just like Famine did before, I drew upon the life force of the plants around us, making the grass turn brown again. The tree over us withered and died, its leaves falling upon us like rain. I gathered all of it inside me, and then I funneled it into Zel.

The magic kicked her own immortal healing into overdrive, and she gasped as her eyes popped open. Her stomach knit back together and color returned to her face, while she stared at me with shock.

"What...?" she asked.

"I'll explain everything later." I stroked her cheek with tears of relief in my eyes. "But if you could stop almost dying on me, that would be great."

She shrugged a little, though it made her wince. "I make no promises."

"My queen, the portal is ready," Mirabella said, from behind me.

"Thank you." I ordered everyone to go through it, while I did my best to repair the area. The spot where I'd healed Zel would never recover though, I feared. It would remain lifeless, a grim memorial to her neath death.

Callan carried her through the portal, and then there were only a few of us left. I glanced back at the tomb and the statue towering over it one last time, feeling a strange mix of affinity and hatred for the place, no doubt from this new part of me that had been trapped there for thousands of years.

Mirabella lightly touched my elbow. "Before you go, I wish to thank you for saving me and Eira from Famine."

I blinked at her. "Eira?"

"Fenrir's daughter, the ice wolf. She's half-fae from the Winter Court. Her mother died when she was a baby, so she was raised by Fenrir among shifters. She was a messenger for the demons like me, and a good friend, at least until Fenrir turned against Lucifer." Her voice trailed off with a hint of sadness. It was a good reminder that this civil war had torn apart our people, and Lucifer and I would have to do a lot of work to heal it, even once we stopped Fenrir. At least Nemesis was gone now.

"I do everything I can to protect my people," I said to Mirabella.

She bowed low, and I turned toward the portal. It was time to get back to Earth to face Lucifer.

To face War.

12

LUCIFER

After realizing the woman and my child were gone, I'd destroyed the penthouse in a rage. I barely remembered any of it, and only came out of my berserker frenzy when Samael and some angels rushed in to try to stop me. How foolish they were, thinking they could stand against me. A touch of my power turned them into mindless warriors craving blood, and now Samael served me once more. As for the angels that were with him, they were chained up in the basement of The Celestial. We'd use them as prisoners of war, or possibly bait, if needed.

I poured myself a drink and stood on the edge of the balcony, gazing down at the city I owned. A city that would soon know bloodshed and terror as the war between angels and demons began once more. Samael was currently rallying our forces, preparing them for battle. Soon the angels would be here too. My blood raced at the thought of the fighting that would soon break out across these brightly-lit streets. I craved the clash of weapons and the spray of blood, the cries of agony and of triumph.

I turned back to look at the destroyed furniture inside my penthouse. The black leather couches and the piano had been familiar to me, bringing back many memories, but other parts of my past were gaping black holes. Now they were in pieces, the leather ripped, the piano smashed. No matter. It was better this way. There wasn't a room in my home that didn't smell of the woman, and her presence invaded me with every breath I drew.

But she wasn't here now. Samael wouldn't tell me where she'd gone either. Somehow he managed to resist that one question, but I would get an answer soon. Those who wouldn't bend to my will would break.

I needed to find the woman and bring her here. Now that I'd kissed her, her absence created a hole in my chest, one I hadn't expected and didn't know how to fill.

As soon as I had that thought, War filled me with fury at the woman for making me feel that way. Now that I'd taken my rightful place as Demon King, I needed nothing and no one but myself. Especially not *her*.

Samael appeared in the entrance of the penthouse. "Lucifer."

"Your king," I corrected him. I gave him a hard look, and he inclined his head.

"My king. A large group of angels is approaching the city."

"Excellent." I downed the rest of my drink. "Are our soldiers ready?"

"Yes, but..." He hesitated, and I felt him fight against my control. "Are you sure this is the best course of action?"

"You dare to question me?" I slammed my empty glass onto the bar, and it shattered in my hand. "The war against the angels never should have ended. I made a mistake when I made peace with them, but the days of peace are over now. We won't stop until they surrender, or we destroy every single one of them."

Samael gave a quick shake of his head but pressed his lips into a line. "Of course, my king."

The bastard was stubborn, no doubt about it, and far too calm for my War powers to incite. But I had other tricks as Lucifer. I hadn't used my persuasive powers on Samael in a very long time, but I couldn't have him questioning me either.

"You followed me when we first left Heaven and made Hell our home. You will follow me again now." I laced power into my words and gave him a cocky smile. "We can't let the angels win after all these years, can we?"

"No, we can't," he murmured. His strength finally gave out against my own, and he bowed his head. "I will follow you anywhere, my king. Even into this war."

"There will be no war," the woman's voice said behind me.

I jerked my head toward the penthouse entrance, where the angel woman known as Hannah stood. Something about her was different, and it took me a moment to realize why—

she emanated the power of an Elder God. How the fuck was that possible?

Three tall, dark-haired men fanned out behind her, and more confusion invaded my mind like there was something I needed to recall. I looked at them closely but they weren't familiar, even though they tugged at my brain like the woman did.

"It's already done," I told her. "War is coming to this city, and then to the rest of the world, and then to every other one. There's nothing you can do to stop it."

"I can stop *you*." She walked toward me, and as she got closer, that ancient, all-consuming power radiated from her. A power I recognized as being akin to my own.

"Famine?" I asked. No, that wasn't right. The angel woman wasn't Famine, yet Famine's power radiated from her, both calling to and repelling War. They were old enemies, and War wanted me to destroy her. *Kill, kill, kill,* he told me over and over. But I couldn't keep my gaze off the angel woman's lips, or the fullness of her breasts and hips, or the slight swell of her stomach where she carried my child. My daughter. I breathed in without thinking, taking a fresh wave of her scent deep inside me.

"I released Famine and became her host, just like you did with War," she said. "But then I took control and I defeated her, claiming her power as my own. You can do this too, Lucifer."

I stared at her, trying to comprehend how this could be possible. I felt the briefest spark of hope, before War trampled it down and raged within me.

Kill her, he ordered.

"Get away from me," I managed to say through gritted teeth, as I glared at the woman. On the inside I was being torn in two, divided by my need to both kill and protect her. "Stay...back..."

"No, I won't do that." She rested a hand on my chest. "War wants to convince you that everything is conflict and anger, but that's not true. Reach deep inside yourself and try to find peace."

I gripped her hand tightly, but couldn't let it go. "There is no peace inside me."

"That's War talking. The man I love has fought for peace for years. He ended the war with the angels. He fought by their side when they were threatened from within."

"I am not this man you speak of."

"You are. You just don't remember because War took your memories of me, and of our children." She turned back to the three men. "Our sons. Belial. Damien. Kassiel."

I cast another glance at them, all looking as if they were ready to attack me and defend their mother should I make a move against her. I was suddenly struck by the sense that they were also my blood, and saw some of my features in their faces reflected back at me. There was no denying the child inside her either. The woman spoke the truth.

"I will kill you all," War forced me to say, as he tried to exert his control again.

"No, you won't," she said. "You'd never hurt them. You might not remember them, but you know them. After all, you became War to save our oldest son, Belial."

I had no memory of what she spoke of, yet somehow I knew it was true. Inside me, War sent rage and hatred through my veins, trying to overwhelm me with bloodlust, but I fought him off. I had to know the truth of what had happened to me. But he was so strong, it seemed impossible to defeat him.

"Lucifer." The woman's voice called me back to her, and she reached up to stroke my face. "You know I'm your mate, deep down, even if you can't remember me. Embrace that feeling. You're not yourself right now. You sacrificed your memories for the good of all of us, but now you need to trust me. Believe in me and in our love. Believe in our family."

I started to shake my head, denying her words. She was nothing to me. Nothing. I was Lucifer, and War, and love did not exist in my world. "No!"

She cupped my cheek and kissed me, her mouth soft and gentle but unrelenting. I gathered her in my arms and returned the pressure, my tongue probing against her mouth. There was something about this woman. I couldn't get close enough.

She pulled back and took my face in her hands, staring into my eyes. "Fight War, Lucifer. You can defeat him. Let me help you."

"I can't. He's too strong."

"You are stronger."

Then she kissed me again, opening her mouth and touching my tongue with hers. Heat sizzled between us and I drew her closer, until we were almost one body. At the same time, I felt some of my anger and rage leeching away from me, along with my life force. Famine's magic stole energy and power, and she took that away from me as her mouth moved across mine.

My hands moved down to cup her stomach, to feel the life growing inside her that I'd helped create. A small little kick answered me in return, like my daughter was reaching out to me, calling for her dad. She needed me, and it gave me all the strength I needed to keep fighting.

War raged inside me, but he was growing weaker as Hannah leeched his rageful energy away. I clung to her, but War wouldn't let this battle end so easily. He suddenly unleashed a wave of frenzied anger, and gargoyles and Fallen rushed into the penthouse to attack my sons. They even came for my woman. My daughter.

"No!" I roared, as I pushed War back down and made the attackers stop. He would not hurt my family. I'd been willing to sacrifice myself, but not them. Never them.

You need me, War said. *I can make you great.*

I'm already great, asshole.

"Focus on peace and love," Hannah's voice said, coming to me through the swirling rage inside my mind that I desperately tried to fight off. "I know you can do this."

I pushed my mate away as my knees buckled, and I clutched my head. "I can't."

She reached for me again and took my hands, holding them in hers as she watched me, her gaze gentle. Pale light began to surround her, something I recognized as the light of truth. An Erelim angel trick. "Remember who you are. Yes, you are the Demon King, but you're also my mate. My husband. My destiny. You're the man who searched for me in every lifetime. Who waited patiently for me to be reborn every time. Who broke the curse and sacrificed himself to save the people he loves. Remember me. Remember *us*."

Her light surrounded me, and it all came back to me like being struck by a lightning bolt. I remembered it all. Eve and Hannah and every other life. Our sons. *Everything*.

I'd stopped the war against angels and fought for peace because of Hannah. Because of my family. Remembering them gave me the final push I needed to fight back against War, to ground him into dust.

He tried to escape my body, probably to find another host, but I latched onto him with my power and kept him inside me. Then I pummeled him with everything I had, until his essence exploded within my body in a flash of angry red hatred.

And then he was gone.

War's voice no longer echoed in my head, and his anger didn't tense my muscles or drive my thoughts any longer. Yet something from him was still inside me, a permanent part of me now.

I was Lucifer, but I was War too.

"Hannah." I captured my mate against me, as relief and love filled my chest. "I knew you would find a way to save me."

"I'm sorry it took so long."

"I'm sorry I tried to kill you."

She smiled up at me and shrugged. "You didn't put much effort into it."

"Is it done?" Belial asked, from behind us. "Are you free?"

I turned toward my sons, my heart swelling at the sight of all three of them together. My family—all here to save me. Including this new gift growing inside Hannah now. "Yes. I'm free."

13

HANNAH

I wrapped my arms around Lucifer and pressed my face against his chest, so relieved to have him back I could barely breathe. I no longer sensed War's presence, and instead felt only the man I'd loved for thousands of years.

He touched my cheek and I looked up at him. Love shone in his eyes, and no trace of War's red, angry glow lingered. Except now he *was* War, just as I was Famine. We'd been many things during my numerous past lives, but this was most unbelievable.

Lucifer turned toward our sons again with a smile. "You're all here. It's been so long."

"I couldn't have saved you without their help," I said, my heart bursting with pride and love. I'd wanted our entire family together again, and now I had my wish. It wasn't going to be the last time it happened either. I'd fought too hard to save Lucifer and bring this family together again, and I was going to keep it intact.

"Thank you," he told them.

"Father, it's been too long." Damien stepped forward and clasped Lucifer's hand as I drew away to allow them to embrace. I'd reunited with my sons, and now it was Lucifer's turn. Kassiel also moved to hug his father, and only Belial hung back, uncertainty in his eyes. But when Lucifer turned to our oldest son, it was with a hint of wry amusement playing at his lips and forgiveness in his gaze. Eventually, Belial stepped forward and shook Lucifer's hand. He said something low, something only meant for his father to hear, and Lucifer nodded.

Then Lucifer turned back to me and pulled me into his arms again. His hand crept lower between us until it rested against my swelling stomach, and his eyes looked at mine with awe. "Another child. I never imagined it might be possible."

I nodded and placed my hands over his. "A daughter, according to Marcus. She's strong too."

"I can tell. Strong like her mother." He looked so happy, but then he sighed. "I've missed so much of your pregnancy. I'm sorry."

"It's not your fault. I only had the first inkling that I might be pregnant when you became War, but I wasn't sure until after we left Heaven and I had Marcus examine me." I hesitated, debating whether to tell him about my sacrifice with Famine, but perhaps that was better saved for a private moment. Instead, I glanced around the penthouse, noting how it had been torn apart while I'd been gone. "What did you do to this place?"

He shrugged. "I destroyed it in a fit of rage when I came back and found you gone."

I sighed. "This poor penthouse. It's been through so much."

Lucifer nodded, his face thoughtful. "Yes, it has. Perhaps it's time to move on from it."

"My king," Samael said, behind us. I'd barely even noticed he was there during all of this.

Lucifer scowled and waved a hand, and Samael's shoulders slumped a little in relief. "There. Now you're no longer under War's—or my—control."

"That's what I wanted to talk to you about," Samael said. "The angels are coming to attack the city. They should be here any minute."

Lucifer swore under his breath. His wings, fully black again with only a slight red aura, unfurled as he turned to me. "It seems I've started a war with the angels, and now I need to put an end to it."

"Of course you did," I said, with a slight shake of my head. "I'm coming with you."

Lucifer took my hand and pressed a kiss to it. "I wouldn't expect anything less, my queen." He turned back to Samael. "Please have all the demons stand down, and try to undo anything else I did when I was War. Kassiel, I locked Olivia and her other men up when I was War, and I apologize for that. Perhaps you and your brothers can free them now."

"We're on it," Kassiel said.

While the others took care of things back at The Celestial, Lucifer and I flew off the balcony and into the night.

My silvery wings also had a barely noticeable green glow radiating from them, the only hint of my new status as an Elder God. Lucifer raised an eyebrow at them and I shrugged, and we held hands as we soared through the crisp night air. Reunited once again, and damn it felt good.

Just outside the city, we found about a hundred angel warriors flying toward Las Vegas over the desert, led by Gabriel. He wore gleaming silver armor and carried a spear, his expression menacing. Something angry lurked in there, something that would only be satisfied by the spilling of blood. Every single angel prepared to attack the second they saw us, but to my relief they waited for Gabriel's command.

"Is this your idea of a battle?" Gabriel called out to Lucifer. "Where are your demonic soldiers? Or is your ego really that large?"

"There will be no battle today," Lucifer said, and then he extended his power outward. "I release you."

The angry haze lifted from Gabriel's eyes and he blinked at us in confusion. "Lucifer? Hannah?"

"I'm sorry, my old friend." Lucifer rested his hand on Gabriel's shoulder. "I was not myself. I do not truly wish for a war with your people."

"Nor do I," Gabriel said, before he turned to face his soldiers. "Stand down! Return to your homes. There will be no fight here today."

The angel warriors all seemed a bit confused, but sheathed their weapons and began flying away. Some looked relieved that they wouldn't spill demon blood today, while others looked disappointed. Soon, only Gabriel remained, the three of us hovering in the air as we faced each other.

Lucifer broke the silence. "You offered me a drink before, and I turned it down. Let me offer you one now."

"I accept," Gabriel said. "I'd love to know how you broke free of War's spell."

The three of us flew back to the penthouse together, our shoes crunching on broken glass and splintered wood as we set down inside our ruined home.

"I'm sorry for the mess," I told Gabriel with a sigh. "Lucifer had something of an anger management problem, but we've taken care of it."

"Where is War now?" Gabriel asked.

"He's gone," Lucifer said, as he poured two drinks from the one liquor bottle that had somehow survived his wrath, plus a glass of water for me.

Gabriel drew his brows together. "How can an Elder God be gone?"

"Famine is gone too," I said. "Although that's not exactly correct."

Lucifer gestured between us. "You're looking at what's left of Famine and War."

"How is that possible?"

I accepted the glass of water from Lucifer. "I released Famine, became her host, and then defeated her."

Gabriel's eyes widened. "I had no idea that could be done."

"Oberon told me it was possible, though he didn't seem to think it would work." I tilted my head as I considered. "I suspect for most people, it wouldn't. I was able to combat Famine because my essence is the opposite of hers. Just like Lucifer's is really the opposite of War's—once he remembered who he truly was." With Famine's added strength and magic, I'd been able to use my Erelim light of truth, boosting it to unheard-of levels in order to bring back Lucifer's memories. I'd never have been able to do that before becoming an Elder God myself—only Famine could weaken War enough for my other powers to succeed.

Gabriel took a sip of his drink with a grin. "Lucifer...a man of peace. Who would have guessed it, all those years ago?"

"Don't spread that rumor around," Lucifer said with a smirk. "I need to keep my villainous image, after all."

"I don't think that will be a problem." Gabriel finished his drink and set his glass down. "I'll leave you two to catch up, while I make sure there are no angels lingering behind with thoughts of taking out a demon or two." He clasped Lucifer on the shoulder. "It's good to have you back."

After he flew away, I turned to Lucifer, relieved to finally have him alone at last. We did have a lot of catching up to do—and many things to discuss.

14

HANNAH

Lucifer took my hands and drew me toward him. "Not a day passed that I didn't think of you, even when I was War. Your face haunted my every thought, though I didn't understand why."

"I thought about you every day also. I felt so guilty for locking you up—"

He placed a finger over my lips."No. You did the right thing."

"I know I did, but I still hated it, and things were so hard without you..."

"Hannah." My name was a soothing caress, as visceral as any touch. He dropped a kiss to my hair and smoothed runaway strands from my face. "From what I've seen and heard, you did an amazing job while I was gone. You stepped up and became queen to our people, all while pregnant. I'm only sad I missed so much."

"You didn't mean to be gone." I laid my hand on his

chest, feeling the reassuring beat of his heart under my palm. "You did what had to be done."

He rumbled a sound that could have been agreement or frustration, then smoothed his hand over my belly. "I'm here now though, and I'm not going anywhere. I'll be by your side every second of these last few months of your pregnancy, until you're begging me to leave you alone. Foot rubs? I'm your man. Strange cravings? Not a problem. Awkward pregnancy sex? Anytime you want."

I laughed a little at that, but then I remembered that this would be the last time we'd be going through all of this. I turned away, my eyes filling with tears, but Lucifer caught my chin.

"What is it?" he asked, his voice full of concern.

"To save you, I had to make a sacrifice too." I swallowed the lump of sadness in my throat.

Horror filled his eyes. "Is something wrong with the baby? Did... Did Famine...?"

I shook my head quickly before he believed the wrong thing. "No, Famine hasn't hurt her. She's just..." I stopped talking, but frown lines formed between Lucifer's brows, and I had to finish before he imagined any worse. "She's the last baby I can have."

He wrapped me in his strong arms, pressing me against his chest. "I'm so sorry, Hannah. I'm so sorry she's taken that from you."

"From us," I mumbled against his shoulder. I held him tight, feeling the sadness deep within my bones as my sacrifice really sank in. Lucifer clung to me too, no doubt feeling his own sorrow and grief.

He pulled back and wiped a tear from my eye. "I'm sorry. I had no idea you'd given up so much to save me."

"I won't lie, it hurts. I'm not sure I even want another child after this one, but to know it's impossible..."

"I understand, and I feel the same."

I tried to smile. "But we have four healthy children, right?"

He nodded, still watching my eyes. "That's an heir and more than enough spares. Of course, our heir tried to overthrow us multiple times, but we have time to work that out with him."

A short laugh escaped me at that. "It was so good to see them all together. We need to keep our family close from now on."

"I've been thinking the same thing. I made so many mistakes with our family before, but things are different now. The curse is broken, and we won't have those long years without you. Our daughter will never have to try to adjust to her mother in a new body, like our sons did."

"No, she won't," I said with relief. "And now that we're Elder Gods we can finally defeat Adam, so he won't ever be a threat to her."

"Adam..." He growled a little at the thought. "He came here as Pestilence while you were gone, but I fought him off. I believe I weakened him, but I'm sure he will be back."

"We'll be ready when he does. We already have a plan in place."

"Of course you do." Lucifer pressed a kiss to my forehead. "I'm constantly amazed at your strength. Every lifetime, you inspire me. But in this one, you've truly outdone yourself, my queen."

"Thank you. You're not so bad yourself, you know." I draped my arms around his neck. "Now, about that awkward pregnancy sex..."

A sexy, masculine sound of amusement rumbled deep in his throat. "Whatever my wife needs."

"Is there anywhere in this penthouse that isn't trashed?" I asked.

He picked me up like I weighed nothing, then carried me into the bedroom we'd once shared, where I'd slept alone for months. The bed remained untouched, still covered in black silk sheets, with my added teal pillows.

"Even in my frenzied state, I couldn't destroy this," Lucifer said, as he set me down on it. His voice was low and deep and sent a shiver of anticipation through me. "Although I'm starting to think maybe we need a new place to live..."

I grabbed his shirt and yanked it open, sending buttons flying. "Stop talking and fuck me already. It's been six months since I've seen you, and these pregnancy hormones have been killer."

He gave me a wicked grin as he removed his shirt, revealing the smooth, muscled chest I'd missed so much. "I used to wait lifetimes for you. Six months is nothing."

I grabbed a pillow and hit him with it. He took it from me and tossed it aside with a chuckle, then pinned me to the bed, taking care not to crush my stomach. His kiss devoured me, while his hands entwined with mine above my head. My body arched toward him, the need to have him fill me so strong I thought I might scream. All I could do was kiss him back harder and rock my hips against him, silently begging him for more.

He rose up, just enough to yank off my shirt and tear off my bra. Then he stared down at me, his fingers brushing over the swell of my body and cupping my breasts. "Incredible."

"There have been some changes while you were gone." I squirmed, midway between embarrassment and amusement.

He met my gaze with a hungry look in his eyes. "I love you like this, round with my child. I'm going to savor every second of it."

"Start now," I murmured, reaching for his pants.

"So impatient," he teased. He unfastened my pants and tugged them off, taking my panties too. I was still wearing the clothes I'd worn to fight Famine in and they were a bit dusty, but none of that mattered to him.

He admired me for a few seconds, then he sank between my legs and kissed the side of my knee, and my breath caught. I anticipated him kissing along the inside of my thigh, but as I held my breath, waiting, he moved away and started at the other knee.

"Like I said, I'm going to savor you."

I huffed but closed my eyes because Lucifer savoring me... I'd missed it.

His fingers gripped the outsides of my thighs as he parted them farther, and my breathing increased just from the anticipation. His tongue touched my skin, and I moved my hands until I pushed them through his thick, dark hair.

I tugged, trying to pull him closer. "Lucifer."

He made that rumble of amusement again, but then he took pity on me and covered my clit with his mouth. I let out a breathy moan at finally getting a sample of what I craved, as his tongue moved across my folds, tasting every inch of me like he couldn't get enough. He buried his face in my pussy, and I lost all thought as he sucked my clit harder. He feasted like a starving man, as if I was the best meal he'd ever had.

"Mmm." He hummed his satisfaction. "You missed me."

"So much." But my words were broken by harsh breaths as his mouth worked magic on me. My hands were back in his hair, tugging at the dark strands, and he responded to me, applying more pressure, licking and sucking harder and faster. Then looked at me, his eyes glowing red, before lowering his head again to flick his tongue over my clit in one possessive stroke. It was enough to send me spinning away from him as all of my muscles tightened and released. I hung in a moment of free fall, my breath held in my chest as I rode the feeling.

My body pulsed and I gasped for air as Lucifer rose up above me with a dark smile. Then he slowly dragged his trousers off, his large, perfect cock jutting forth with obvious need. I wasn't the only one dying for release here.

I sat up a little and took his cock into my mouth, just for

a few seconds, unable to help myself. I needed to taste him too. He caught his breath, and I relished my small degree of control over this man who was used to controlling every other element of his life. Here, he was mine.

"Fuck, I missed you too," he said, as he gripped my head lovingly. But then his need overwhelmed him too and he let out a groan and jerked his cock out of my mouth.

He laid back on the bed and pulled me on top of him, making me straddle him. With fingers digging into my hips, he lifted me up while looking me in the eyes, his intense and glowing red. I wondered if mine were glowing too, but that was my last thought before I sank down, sliding him inside me.

It felt amazing, both of us joined together at last. I wasn't sure if it was because I was pregnant or because we were both gods now, but I felt him so much more than I ever had before, both physically and on a spiritual level. Our souls were entwined, just as our bodies were.

"You feel so good." Lucifer groaned, a deep sound that vibrated right through both of us. His hands were on my hips, before he ran them over my ribs and to my breasts, touching me everywhere, like he'd never felt me before. Then he thrust up hard, filling me so deeply it made me gasp. It was exactly what my body needed though, and now I wanted more.

At first Lucifer let me set my own rhythm as he fondled my breasts, watching them bounce over him, and I threw my head back and enjoyed the pleasure building within me. I rode him harder and faster, and I loved the feel of his cock sliding deeper into me with each thrust. But then his hands returned to my hips and he growled as he began to thrust up, matching me, holding me at the angle he wanted, fucking me harder and faster like he couldn't get enough.

He reached up to tangle his hand in my hair and pulled my face down to his, kissing me in a way that left no doubt that I belonged to him. His possessive fucking only fueled my own desire, and I let go and allowed him to take control of my body completely. I melted into him as we moved as one, each of his thrusts teasing more heat through me until I screamed his name and dug my nails into his skin, shouting my pleasure. As the orgasm rocked through me, power erupted out of me, and then Lucifer's breathing changed and he joined me with his own rush of energy. Glass shattered around us, but I barely noticed as he thrust a few last times, dragging out the moment where we'd never been more connected.

As my throbbing body returned to gentle flutters, I fell over his chest, rolling slightly to the side to allow for my cumbersome shape. Then I noticed the plants growing all over the room, which I must have created when he made me climax. Oops. Lucifer's orgasm had demolished more of the penthouse too, destroying what little had still been standing.

He followed my gaze and raised an eyebrow. "That's new."

"Was it just me, or was sex even more intense as an Elder God?"

"I'm not sure," he rumbled, as he reached down to slide a finger inside me. "I think we should do it again to be sure."

"Already?"

"Definitely." He grabbed me and set me on my knees, then mounted me from behind. His cock was already hard and pushing against my entrance, begging for entry. "After all, we have six months to make up for...and I have the stamina of a god."

After that, there were no more words as I pushed back against his cock, taking him in deep, while he reached forward and grabbed my hair to yank my head back. He took me hard and fast, like he would die if he didn't claim every inch of me—but we were gods now and nothing could harm me. I reveled in every second of it, until he had me screaming his name again and tightening around his cock, squeezing out his own climax while our power shook the entire floor of the penthouse.

"If we keep this up, we might need to move," I said, as my body trembled under the lingering effects of my last orgasm.

"I've been thinking the same thing." He wrapped me up in his arms and kissed me. "But right now all that matters is we're together—and nothing is going to tear us apart ever again."

15

LUCIFER

I glanced at the pile of books on the desk again. Hannah had left no stone unturned, no tome unopened. There were books open I doubted she could even understand, but I could imagine her taking her time turning the fragile pages looking for a familiar word or a diagram in a margin. How often had she spent late nights in this room searching for the way to rescue me from War's clutches?

I didn't need an answer. Instinct told me she'd made every night a late one during her search. Somehow she'd risen to Demon Queen during my absence as well, all while pregnant—and pretty ill too, from what I'd gathered.

I'd always known Hannah would rescue me. It was one of the reasons I'd taken such a risk in the first place. But seeing the evidence of all her hard work made me appreciate her efforts even more.

I breathed in the scent of my library—the ancient pages, the leather chairs, and now the slight floral scent from

Hannah's plants. Though I'd destroyed much of the penthouse when I was War, I'd left enough of this space untouched for me to work at my desk for a few hours, trying to catch up on everything I'd missed in the last six months.

I'd missed a lot, it seemed. Time hadn't passed the same for me with War in my body. I hadn't thought about normal things or needed to eat or sleep. I'd had two focuses.

One, escape the confines of Heaven. Two, bring war and chaos to the world.

Hannah stepped into the library, absolutely glowing in a pale green floor-length dress that showed off her rounded belly. Pride and love filled me, and I immediately stood and crossed the library to her, taking her in my arms. I'd never truly felt lucky before. Certainly not like this.

"Hello, my love. How are you feeling this morning?" I asked, as I drew her against me.

"Strange. I don't need to sleep or eat anymore...but I still like to do both of those things." She shrugged. "How are you?"

"I'm brilliant. Never better." I pressed a kiss to her forehead. "Is it time for the meeting?"

"I believe it is."

"Come with me?" I lowered my voice and spoke against her ear. "We'll have time to nap later."

She rolled her eyes. "Of course I'm coming to the meeting. I can't let you loose with my Archdemons until I see that you know what you're doing."

"Oh, they're your Archdemons now?" I took her hand and led her out of the library, excited to be sharing my throne after so many lifetimes I'd spent without her. "I see how it is—I leave you alone for a few months and you take over completely."

"What's that saying? What's yours is mine, and what's mine is mine..."

"That does sound like marriage, yes."

As we held hands and grinned at each other like young lovers, we took the elevator down a level, to the command center. The demons working there bowed and some even clapped as we entered, and I gave them all a cocky grin and a little wave, though Hannah shook her head at me. It never hurt to remind them that I really did live up to all the stories about me.

We stepped into the conference room, where our allied Archdemons were waiting for us, along with Samael. They all rose to their feet when we entered, and Lilith actually rushed forward and threw her arms around me. Then she hugged Hannah next.

"You did it," she said. "You actually managed to save him."

"She did," I confirmed, with a wry smile at my wife. "I owe my salvation to Hannah, though I would like to thank each and every one of you for your part in keeping the demon world running smoothly over the last few months. Romana, thank you for your loyalty and for your people's help in guarding Hannah. Baal, I truly appreciate the risks you've taken in spying on Nemesis and Fenrir for me. Lilith, Hannah's told me your counsel and support were invaluable to her, and I thank you for that."

"I think I speak for everyone when I say it was an honor to help however we could," Lilith said. "However, we're all relieved you've returned to us."

"As am I. I thank you all for your loyalty during this difficult period, though there is one more person I must thank—Samael." I turned to my oldest, dearest friend. "You've supported me through all these years, and when I was gone, you stood by Hannah's side in my absence."

"I did what anyone would do in such a position," he said, his voice deep yet humble.

"No, you always manage to go above and beyond, my friend." I rested a hand on his shoulder, and he stoically nodded, though I can see in his eyes that he was pleased.

"Is it true you're both really Elder Gods?" Romana asked. "What happened to War? And Famine?"

"Yes, it's true," Hannah said.

"You could say we defeated them...and then took their place," I added.

"They're truly gone then?" Baal asked.

Hannah's eyes grew sympathetic. "I'm sorry. If I could have done it without defeating your mother, I would have. If it makes you feel better, she seemed to still care for you, in her own way."

He held up a hand. "Do not apologize. It's actually a relief to know she's gone. I no longer have to live in fear of my mother awakening and destroying the world."

I knew exactly how he felt—except my father, Death, was still out there, locked away in his tomb, waiting to be set free. With Famine released, we were one stepped closer to his awakening, and that thought terrified me like nothing else.

"Nemesis is dead too," Hannah said. "I killed her in the battle in Faerie at Famine's tomb. Unfortunately, Fenrir got away."

"Do you think he'll go after Death next?" Romana asked.

"Possibly, if he's still stupid and stubborn enough to continue this battle," I said.

"He is," Baal confirmed.

"Even so, he can't get into Hell, where Death's tomb is located," Lilith said. "Lucifer made sure of that when he sealed that realm up all those years ago. Only he and I have the keys."

"A good point." I turned to Samael. "Let's make sure to get extra protection on Lilith."

"That's not necessary," Lilith said.

"No, he's right." Baal took her hand, and I noticed Samael narrowing his eyes. "We must protect that key at all costs."

"What of Pestilence?" Romana asked.

The very thought of him made me bristle. "When I was War I fought him and weakened him, but I have no doubt he'll be back."

"We already have a plan in place for Pestilence's return.' Hannah looked at me as she spoke, then turned to the table. "But I think we should have something else ready if it doesn't work."

"Somehow I doubt Adam has any interest in fighting off Pestilence's control, like you two did," Samael said.

"No, that won't work. We need another plan." Hannah turned to me. "Oberon said you once had a key to Void. Do you still have it?"

A chill ran down my spine. Whatever I'd expected her to say, it hadn't been that. "We're not using that."

"But you've been to Void before," Baal said.

"Yes, thousands of years ago, and I risked a lot by asking Nyx to make the Fallen into demons so they could survive in Hell. I'm lucky I made it back at all."

"How did you even get such a thing?" Romana asked.

"My father, Death, gave it to me. Before we became bitter enemies."

"It might work," Samael said, his voice thoughtful. "The key is the only thing that can send the Elder Gods to the Void."

I cast a hard look around the table at my allies. "Yes, but opening a portal to Void could also let other Elder Gods out. We don't need any more of them on our hands, now do we?"

They all murmured their agreement, and I considered the matter dropped, but I sensed they were all still wary. They wanted an easy solution, but when facing threats such as these, there wasn't one. It was always a matter of choosing the best option between multiple shitty situations, then praying you made the right decision.

I rose to my feet, forcing them to look up at my full height as I towered over them like the king I was. "Now that Hannah and I have the powers of War and Famine, Pestilence won't be able to stand against us. In the meantime, use all of our resources to hunt down Fenrir. I want him brought to justice immediately."

Hannah looked at me and nodded, before I sat beside her again—in my rightful place as Demon King.

Damn, it was good to be back.

16

HANNAH

As we stepped through the archway that led to Persephone's Garden, the first hint of nervousness took root in my chest. Lucifer had given me this space six months ago, back when it was nothing more than an empty lot and a dream. He'd known I would miss the flower shop and would need a connection to nature even in the middle of the Nevada desert. But then he was gone, and I'd had to design and implement the garden all by myself, trying to make it a place that the guests of The Celestial Resort & Casino would enjoy. Now I dearly wished for his approval.

It had been two days since Lucifer had become himself again and things were starting to feel normal once more. Azazel had fully recovered, thanks to my gift of energy, followed by Marcus's healing. Belial and Damien were staying in the hotel for now, though I doubted they would stay for long. The meeting with the Archdemons had gone well, and Lucifer and I were getting used to being Elder

Gods. There were definitely some benefits to not needing any sleep.

Lucifer held my hand as he let me lead the way through the winding paths, under the dense trees and past the perfectly arranged plants toward the waterfall. "It's gorgeous."

"You like it?" I asked, turning a big smile on him. The sound of the waterfall soothed me instantly, and I inhaled the sweet fragrances of the flowers.

He nodded and raised my hand to his mouth, brushing his lips over my knuckles. "It's beautiful. Just as I knew it would be. As all your gardens have been."

"I was nervous doing it without your approval since this hotel is your baby," I said, as I walked to my bench. After I sat, I patted the smooth stone beside me. "This is my favorite spot."

"Might be my favorite spot, too." He grinned and sat as close to me as he could, pulling me into his arms. He dipped his head and kissed my neck, a promise of more to come. "You didn't need my approval. You had my complete faith when I gave you the project."

I arched my neck to grant him better access to my skin. "I know, but it would have been nice to be able to run decisions by you first..."

"I doubt I would have been much help. You know I'm not good with all this...nature. I leave that to you."

I rolled my eyes. It was true, Lucifer couldn't name any of the flowers near us if he'd tried. He was completely useless in that area. "We're hoping to open it to hotel guests next week."

"They're going to love it. It's really going to elevate the hotel's profile."

I practically beamed with pride at his comments, but then I noticed his frown as he stared at the waterfall. "What is it?"

"I can't believe I'm saying this, but I think we should move away from Las Vegas." He looked out over the garden like he could see the city itself through the foliage. "I love the very air here. It's saturated in sin, but I want to concentrate on you, and on our daughter."

I leaned against him, finding that spot on his chest that seemed to have been made just for me to snuggle against. "I've been thinking the same thing. We need a fresh start. The Celestial is great and all, but a casino is not the best place to raise a child."

"No it's not, and I'd like to move somewhere safer, and more easily defensible." He gave a rueful glance up at the building. "Those damn floor-to-ceiling windows."

I let out a laugh. "I know! We must have spent a small fortune repairing them over the last year or two."

"It's like no one knows how to use a door anymore," he muttered.

"Including you!"

"That doesn't count. I wasn't in my right mind then."

I stared at the waterfall as I voiced the secret dream I'd had over the last few months, one I'd been scared to even really consider since I didn't know if I'd be able to get

Lucifer back. "While you were away, Asmodeus bought Brandy a house on the beach in southern California. I was thinking I'd like to live near her, since I miss her a lot, and she's pregnant too. We could raise our kids together." Then the hope faded as the reality of the situation hit me again. "But I also don't want to put her or her family in any danger. You and I are always going to be Lucifer and Hannah, Demon King and Queen, War and Famine. We're never going to have a quiet life."

"No, although at the moment that sounds lovely." He stared at the waterfall for a few moments, then turned back to me. "We should do it. We'll always have duties and responsibilities, and there will always be some danger, but we deserve happiness too. As for Brandy and her family, we'll make sure they are well-protected at all times."

Could we really make it work? I wasn't sure. While Lucifer had been gone, it felt like everything in the demon world was so precarious, like it could all easily crumble to dust if I wasn't there to hold it together. But maybe if we managed to stop Pestilence and Fenrir things would calm down for a while. We'd be able to step back from the demon world, delegate more to our Archdemons, and enjoy a small amount of peace. I could dream, anyway.

A soft whinnying sound caught my attention, and we turned to see our two spectral horses moving through the grass. My ever-present gargoyle guards drew their weapons, but I held out a hand to show them this wasn't a threat. War's horse was red and huge, both beautiful and terrifying at once, though he no longer left fiery hoof prints behind him. Mine was smaller and jet black, with a luxurious mane that blew gently in the breeze.

"Where did they come from?" I asked.

Lucifer took my hand as we rose to our feet and walked over to the horses. "I'm not sure, but they will vanish when not needed. Perhaps they live in the Void and can cross over somehow."

"That's so strange."

"The strangest thing for me was that Strife was the only one I could speak with the whole time I was locked in Heaven." He greeted his horse like a long-lost friend. "Not that he ever said much back, but I enjoyed his company nonetheless."

The red horse nuzzled against Lucifer's hand, and I reached out to touch mine more tentatively. Her coat was smooth and clean, and I ran my hand over it, wondering what it would be like to ride her. She had no saddle, but I had memories of riding horses in various past lives, though I was surely out of practice now. I was tempted to climb onto her back, but I was pregnant. Then again, I was also a Horseman now, and somehow I knew I wouldn't fall off this horse that I was bonded to on a spiritual level.

"My horse is named Misery, though I'm not sure how I know that," I said. "We've only met once so far, right after I became Famine. I'm not sure what I'm supposed to do with her. Did I need to feed her? Brush her? House her?"

"They're Elder Gods themselves, in a way," Lucifer said. "Or maybe they're part of our own essence. I don't really know. Either way, they don't need to eat or sleep, just like we don't, though they might enjoy a good brushing now and then."

"I guess we're bound to them for the rest of time," I said. "If we get a new place to live, we should make sure there's a space for them."

Lucifer patted his horse with a smile. "We should go for a ride sometime. The only thing I enjoyed while in Heaven was riding Strife—he's faster than even I can fly."

"Good idea. Out in the desert sometime maybe?"

Our conversation was interrupted by a scream outside the garden, over by one of the hotel's pools. Lucifer and I were instantly on alert, and my gargoyle guard surrounded us with weapons drawn and their bat-like wings already out. When we rushed toward the sound, we were met by Azazel, her weapons drawn.

"It's Pestilence," she said. "He's here."

17

HANNAH

A ripple of fear went through me, but I kept calm and nodded. I'd prepared for this, and I just had to make sure everything went according to plan. "Sound the alarm and have everyone get into position!"

"What's the plan?" Lucifer asked. We hadn't had time to go over it yet—we'd thought we would have a few weeks before Pestilence returned, at least.

"Just follow my lead." I didn't really have time to explain, not when Pestilence was on his sickly white horse, trotting around the large sparkling blue pool that had dozens of guests in or around it. Now they were either screaming and running, or falling to the ground sick—or worse. A few dead bodies already floated in the pool, and I swallowed hard at the sight of them. Pestilence laughed as he spread more sickness out in a putrid cloud and my hatred for him only increased, which I didn't think was possible.

My gargoyle guards rushed to form a barrier in front of

Pestilence, their stone skin protecting them from his deadly plague, and that allowed a few more of the tourists to escape. What we didn't expect was that Pestilence wasn't alone this time—he'd brought a group of imps and shifter allies, and they all radiated disease like some sort of super-spreaders as they chased down other unsuspecting humans.

"He could infect the whole Strip if we don't stop him!" Lucifer said, as he summoned his War sword of hellfire and darkness and wielded it in front of him.

"I need to get Pestilence back into the garden," I said. "You take care of the others."

Without even stopping to question what I had planned, Lucifer altered his trajectory and headed toward the imps and shifters. I trusted him to take care of them, and I walked toward Pestilence slowly, hoping the others were already moving into position at the waterfall, or this plan would fail. The being that had once been Adam turned his attention toward me, a smile spreading over his sickly yellow face, one of the boils on his chin pulsing like it had a heartbeat.

"Eve, my love." His voice had changed, no longer the sound of my first husband's voice, but now tinged with something far more ancient. His eyes were all white, no pupils at all, and it was hard not to look away when he stared at me with them. "You've changed."

"I wanted to be like you." I took another step forward and let my Famine essence unfurl. My body glowed with a faint green light, and I would bet money that my eyes did too. "Your equal."

He cocked his head. "You released Famine?"

"Yes and I made the sacrifice." It was hard not to gag as I approached him. "Now we can be together. All we have to do is take out War."

He rubbed his hands together. "Yes, and then we can rule this world side by side as gods. That's all I ever wanted."

"I know." I forced a smile. "Come, let me show you my horse, Misery. She's in the garden waiting for me. We can talk more there."

Pestilence dismounted his own horse and sent it away with a gesture. The white beast rode away, turning incorporeal and running over the pool before vanishing. Then the rotting corpse-like Horseman walked alongside me, while my gargoyles hung back, though it clearly pained them to do so. I eyed Adam closely, wondering how he had become so far gone. Lucifer had changed too, with the red angry glow always bursting out of his skin, but he hadn't lost himself as much as Adam had—he must have been fighting War's influence even without his memories of me. I wondered what horrible thing I would have become had I failed to defeat Famine—probably some gaunt, haggard figure with sagging boobs and jagged fangs, always trying to find my next meal. I shuddered a little at the thought.

No one stopped us as we entered Persephone's Garden, and I led Pestilence toward the waterfall. Now that I'd let my Famine powers out, they begged to drain all the life from the plants in the garden, but I held myself back.

"What made you change your mind?" Adam asked.

"When Lucifer became War he was lost to me. He

forgot who I was." I cast a glance over at Adam. "You would never do that."

"No. Never. Over hundreds of years, I always found you. Even when he didn't."

"I know. I became Famine because she has the power to stop War—and so I could be a Horseman like you." I gestured at Misery up ahead, who stood beside the waterfall. "Ah, there's my horse now."

As we approached the waterfall, my gargoyle guard moved in close, with Theo at the lead. Pestilence jerked his head around, just as Belial, Kassiel, and Damien emerged from the hidden cave below the water.

"What's this?" Adam asked.

"It's time for you to go back to sleep." I still had the powers I'd accessed in Faerie, and they were stronger here in the garden I'd created. At my thought, vines wound around Pestilence, binding his limbs, and his face contorted.

"You can't hold Pestilence!" As he spoke, he struggled, and the vines started to wither and die from his poison.

I drew on Famine, finding the vacuum always in the center of me, the one always hungry for power. I focused on Pestilence, drawing on him, taking his energy away. Making him weak.

He screamed as he realized what was happening. "What are you doing? You lied to me!"

"And it was all too easy... You'd think you would know by now that I will never be yours."

Out of the corner of my eye I saw Lucifer flying just outside the garden. He had the imps and shifters fighting each other with a touch of his War frenzy, while Belial and Azazel picked them off on the sidelines and protected the innocent humans. It was almost beautiful as Lucifer moved his hands like the world's most violent conductor. Then he finished his orchestral movement by destroying them with darkness and hellfire. Perfect takedown.

And my cue to finish what I'd started with Pestilence.

I directed the vines to pull Adam under the waterfall, using the walkthrough feature I'd installed. Theo hit a hidden button and the wall slid open to reveal Pestilence's tomb. I'd had it brought here from Stonehenge, banking on the fact Adam wouldn't be able to leave me alone and would return again. And where Adam went, Pestilence went too.

Damien was already inside, with the tomb open and ready. He'd told me it wouldn't work as well the second time around, since the runes weren't fresh—whatever that meant. I had to take the chance though. We had no other option.

Pestilence struggled and glared at me. "No! You will die!"

He sent out wave after wave of disease and horror, but my gargoyle guards were immune and they blocked me from it. Still, it took all of my power to drag him to the tomb, and even then I wasn't sure it would be enough.

With a roar, Adam suddenly broke free of his vines, then materialized a golden bow and arrow and began shooting me with them. One hit my arm and made me instantly feel sick, and I yanked it out and prayed whatever it was wouldn't harm the baby. I knocked him back with a blast of air, then used a weave of darkness and light to shield myself from more arrows.

Just when I thought Adam might actually break free, Lucifer rushed in and tackled him, knocking him backward.

"Get in that tomb, you bastard." Lucifer's face twisted with rage—fury created by all the times Adam had wronged us over the years. He shoved Adam hard, and they both fell into the tomb and began wrestling. Lucifer launched himself out a second later, his body covered in boils from Pestilence's magic, and then blasted Adam with bright blue hellfire. Belial joined in with his own hellfire from the other side of the cave, and I used a combination of vines and air to lift the lid of the tomb and use it to cover Adam.

The second it was closed, Damien spilled his fae blood on top of it, and the runes began to glow. The lid buckled and nearly came off as Pestilence struggled, and Belial rushed forward to add his own. I created a blade of darkness and sliced my own hand, then Lucifer did the same. Angel, demon, human, fae—all represented in our family line. As soon as all the blood mingled, the runes flashed bright, and the tomb sealed. Then it all went dark in the cave.

"Is it done?" Belial asked.

"Yes, but the seal won't last for thousands of years like the previous one did," Damien said. "And I think anyone powerful enough could open it, if they tried."

"But it will hold for now, right?" I asked.

Damien inspected the runes. "Yes, I believe it will hold for at least a decade or two, assuming no one tampers with it."

"That's enough time for us to find a better solution." Lucifer wrapped an arm around me. "An excellent plan, my love."

"Thank you, but it wouldn't have worked without everyone doing their part." My shoulders sagged in relief as I leaned against him. Adam was locked away, and couldn't harm me anymore—or my daughter. We might actually be able to have something akin to a normal life.

For a while, anyway.

18

HANNAH

The next morning I sat in my garden on my bench, gathering my thoughts. We'd cleaned up everything from Pestilence's attack, and the angels had been able to heal most of the hotel guests. Unfortunately, many others were killed during the attack, and Lucifer had to use his persuasive powers to cover it up so it wasn't all over the news. We planned to offer compensation to each family that had lost someone, since it was our fault they'd been attacked at all. It definitely pushed me more in favor of moving out of the city to somewhere more remote, where we wouldn't put so many innocent lives in danger.

The good news was that our plan worked, and Pestilence was securely locked away beneath the waterfall. I felt his power emanating softly throughout the area, and I was certain the humans did too, because it seemed to draw them to The Celestial—and to the garden. His ancient power lured them in without harming them, just as it had done when he was under Stonehenge. A strange benefit of him being locked there, since it would only bring us more business. About time Adam did something that helped us after all these years.

My horse suddenly appeared and approached me. I held my hand out to her and stroked over her face. The horse harrumphed softly, blowing warm air from her nostrils.

"Misery," I murmured, as I took in her black velvet coat, inky with a darkness I almost couldn't define. "One day we'll ride."

Lucifer had ridden his horse all over Heaven and much of Earth, too. Part of me longed to experience that freedom for myself, and I patted Misery again. The two of us were stuck with each other for the rest of eternity it seemed, so I'd better get used to her.

I tiled my head as I stared into her dark eyes. "I think we need a better name for you. Something not quite so dreary."

Misery whinnied softly at that, and I felt something like approval through our strange connection. I didn't get words from her, nothing like that, just a little hint of her thoughts and emotions.

"Blackie? Midnight? Ghost?"

She didn't like any of those. I was pondering some others, when a movement from the nearby olive trees drew my attention. I rose to my feet, but I wasn't worried. Security had been increased even more since Pestilence had been locked up in the garden, and I was well guarded today.

I smiled as Damien strode from the olive trees, something I'd planted because they reminded me of our home in

Faerie. My handsome middle son was a perfect mix of fae and Fallen, and I desperately wanted to spend some time with him after all these years.

"Hello, Mother," he said as he approached with a sad smile.

I stood and held out my hands to him. "Is everything all right?"

"It's been nice being here with all of you, but I must return to Faerie to continue my work. I think I've done all I can here." His gaze drifted to the waterfall and the cave beyond.

"I understand, and I appreciate everything you've done. Before you go, can you sit for a while?" I dropped as gracefully as I could back on the stone bench and patted the space next to me. "It's been a long time since we've caught up properly, and I've only just found you again."

My chest tightened a little at the thought. Thanks to the curse, and then Jophiel hiding who I was for so long, I hadn't seen Damien in years. I'd managed to reconnect with my other sons a little, but it was always a bit awkward. They weren't the men I remembered, and I wasn't the mother they knew. But it was important for me to try, especially with a new addition to our family on the way. I didn't want to be a stranger to any of my sons ever again.

"Yes, I have some time." He sat beside me and gazed across the space. "This garden is lovely. It reminds me of our Spring Court residence."

I beamed at his compliment. "That's exactly what I was trying to emulate, using everything I remembered from my time there. Although when we went to Faerie to release Famine, I realized it would be impossible to truly copy such a place on Earth. This was the best I could do."

"Do you miss Faerie?"

"Sometimes, but it was so many lifetimes ago..." I shrugged. "I have a connection with all the realms, but my place is here on Earth at the moment."

"And mine is in Faerie. Though I hope to be able to visit you more often now. A baby sister is a good excuse, after all. Speaking, of how's my sister doing in there?" He nodded at my stomach and I automatically passed my hand over my bump, happy when my daughter kicked in response.

"She's great. Famine promised she'd come to no harm, and she hasn't."

"I can't wait to meet her. I'll make sure to come back after she's born. I just can't be away from Faerie too long."

"Lucifer told me about the work you're doing there," I said. Damien was pretending to be one of Oberon's most loyal princes, but in truth he was spying on the High King for Lucifer.

Damien nodded, his face serious. "Oberon has kept Faerie neutral for years, but I'm sure he is plotting something big, though I don't know what."

"Is it true he killed Titania?" I asked. Though I'd never been close to the Queen, she had been my aunt, after all.

He glanced around and lowered his voice. "No one can prove it, but everyone knows he did."

"How did my mother..." I paused and started again. "How did Demeter take her sister's death?"

"Not well, but as Queen of the Spring Court she can't openly do anything against Oberon. I'm pretty sure she would act against him if she could though. I've been trying to find others who might help overthrow him someday."

I lifted an eyebrow. "That sounds dangerous."

He shrugged. "Yes, but someone needs to protect the future of Faerie."

I squeezed his arm gently. "Just be careful, okay?"

He rolled his eyes and grinned at me. "I am, don't worry."

"I always worry. That's what mothers do." I reached up to touch his shiny blue-black hair, which was stunningly beautiful under the sun. "What of love? Any special men or women? If I remember correctly, you were quite the charmer as Dionysus. The stories about your parties were legendary. Why don't you use that name anymore?"

He coughed and jerked his head away. "That was the old me. I've changed a lot in the last few thousand years."

"What happened?" I asked, hearing the touch of sadness in his voice. Like most immortals who'd lived thousands of years, he'd gone by many names during his lifetime. Dionysus had been his fae name, and Damien his demon one. I was surprised he used the demon one now, despite living in Faerie.

"After you—Persephone—died..." He paused, as if finding the right words. "Things were different. Belial left Hell, then tried to overthrow Father. I tried to stay out of it, and at first, I threw myself into the parties, booze, and orgies, but later I realized it was just a way to numb myself to the pain of it all. Eventually, I chose a different path."

It pained me to see my most carefree and jovial son so heavy-hearted. While I'd been alive, his life had been a celebration of wine, sex, and merriment. He'd once been a great actor and patron of the theater too, but I supposed now he used those skills as a spy. "Belial told me you both blamed your father for my death."

"It was a difficult time for both of us. I'm not sure I ever told you this, but Belial and I were the ones who found you dead, after Plutus and Philomelus killed you."

That was unusual—normally the curse had me die in Lucifer's arms, but there were a few exceptions, and it probably pleased Death to bring misery upon my sons too.

Plutus had been Adam's incarnation while I'd been Persephone. He was an Autumn Court fae, along with his brother Philomelus, who'd gone along with everything horrible Plutus had done. Recently Philomelus had been helping Adam release Pestilence and War, but I bested him during the battle in Heaven, and Azazel got in the killing blow.

"If it makes you feel any better, Philomelus is dead. And Adam..." I gestured toward the waterfall. "But why did you blame your father?"

"You were killed on one of your trips to Faerie as part of Lucifer's deal with Demeter to spend half your time in Hell, and half there. You tried to get him to go with you, but Lucifer refused, saying he had to stay and rule the demons from the palace in Hell. He always hated going to Faerie, so you went alone—and because of that, you died."

As Damien fell quiet, I smoothed a hand over his back.

"It wasn't Lucifer's fault. It was Adam, and the curse. But that's over now."

"You were safer in Hell," Damien muttered. "Father should have broken the deal with Demeter and kept you there. Or gone with you at least."

I sighed. "Yes, probably, but it's easy to look back at the past and think of all the things we could have done differently. Trust me, with hundreds of past lives and just as many gruesome deaths, I could chase those thoughts for hours. But at some point we have to accept the mistakes we made and try to move forward."

"I know, and I did. I didn't speak with Father for a long time, but eventually I stopped blaming him for what happened. I don't think Belial has ever forgiven him though." He patted my hand. "Maybe he'll come around now."

"Yeah, maybe." But I couldn't help but worry he might not.

"A new sister will help with that. Father and I reconnected a lot after Kassiel was born, mostly thanks to you. That's when I offered to work for him as a spy."

I smiled at the memories of my life as Lenore, one of my last few moments of happiness with my family before recent events. "Yes, I remember."

"Do you?" Damien cocked his head as he studied me.

"When Lucifer broke the curse, all my memories came back. I remember almost everything, though it comes and goes, as memories do."

"Everything? Like the time when I nearly fell into the fire pit?"

I arched an eyebrow. "You mean when Belial was supposed to be watching you?"

He laughed at that. "And all the times you caught me in bed with someone?"

I groaned and ducked my head. "Unfortunately, yes. Both men and women. Sometimes both at the same time. Things a mother should never have to see."

Damien only laughed harder, and I was happy to see some of my old mischievous, carefree son back again. We chatted a bit more about memories of the past, laughing and smiling as we reminisced together. He caught me up a bit more on his life in Faerie, and how he had won over Oberon after many years, and how his grandmother continues to be a thorn in his side even though she obviously cares. I told him more about this life, and everything Jophiel had done to keep me safe from Adam, and how Lucifer broke the curse. But eventually the hour grew late, and it was time to say goodbye.

Damien glanced toward the setting sun. "I should go."

"Do you really have to?"

"Unfortunately yes, but I will be back soon. I promise." He pulled me into a last hug before he opened a portal to Faerie, and I breathed deep at the smell of home that emanated from it.

"You better."

I gave him another hug, and then held back tears as he

disappeared inside the portal, though I was confident I would see him again soon.

Time had been tough on our family, but I was certain that things would be better going forward. I was going to make sure of it.

19

LUCIFER

I looked out over one of the crowded bar areas on the first floor of the Celestial. Tourists came here to drown their sorrows after losing too much money on the slots. Funny how humans continued their lives oblivious to all else going on around them, truly blinded to anything outside their own sphere of understanding. Clinking glasses, chatter and laughter formed the soundtrack to the evening and a sports event flickered on a television just barely in view, tucked around a corner. But none of that interested me.

I peered deeper into the shadows, and there he was. Belial. Alone on a stool and in the furthest reaches of the bar, almost as if he'd set a warded circle around himself to keep people away.

I started to stride over to him, but stopped a short distance away, unsure of my welcome. He looked up, amusement flashing briefly through his eyes as he witnessed my hesitation. I grinned and nodded brief acknowledgment. Yes, any sort of hesitation was uncharacteristic of me, but in this instance, it wasn't weakness. It was the closest I'd come to asking him for consent to join him, and he was too like me to not know that.

He glanced at the barstool next to him. Just a flicker. If I'd have blinked, I'd have missed the invitation, but I'd known not to blink. Belial wouldn't ask twice.

"Drink?" I asked. When had I last bought my son a drink? For that matter, had I ever bought one for him? Of course, I wouldn't actually buy one now either. I'd just wave, and a bartender would keep them coming.

My oldest son lifted his glass, the ice chinking softly inside. "Got one."

I waved anyway. This wasn't a conversation to have without the accompanying burn of good quality whiskey. "How are you doing?"

He answered my uninspired question with a dry, humorless chuckle. "Small talk, really?"

"We've got to start somewhere, don't we?" This was our first real conversation in centuries. I had no idea how to begin it, but I couldn't let things go on this way any longer.

"All right then." He raised an eyebrow, and for a second he looked so much like his mother when she'd been Eve. "I'm just dandy. How are you?"

His voice was dripping with sarcasm. This was never going to be an easy conversation, and I hadn't expected Belial to make it any easier. Still, he could help me out a little here. My whiskey arrived at that moment, and I took a long sip of liquid courage.

"I want to thank you for helping your mother in Faerie. She says she couldn't have done it without you."

Belial simply nodded and sipped his drink. I dragged a hand through my hair, trying to find the right words to connect with my son. This was much harder than I'd expected.

"I'm sorry." I blurted out the words in my head. They weren't the words I'd intended to say, and Belial stiffened, tension in all of his muscles. His head moved toward me almost as if he might look at me, but it was little more than a twitch he didn't complete in the end.

I laughed, the sound self-deprecating. "I realize those aren't words you're used to hearing from me."

He acknowledged me with a quick contraction of his lips, but he still didn't look in my direction as I studied his profile.

"I know I wasn't the best father to you. I was…" I paused, my mouth dry. I'd been about to say I'd been busy, but that wasn't right. "I was stupid."

Belial cut a glance toward me, and it was all the invitation I needed to keep speaking.

"When you were born, I'd just left Heaven to become king of Hell. You were only a baby when I begged Nyx to turn the Fallen into demons. Then a small child when we defeated the Elder Gods and locked away the Horsemen. Then a teenager when Adam killed your mother the first time as part of the curse. I spent your entire childhood struggling to prove myself as the Demon King and to keep the denizens of Hell in line. But I should have spent it with you." I sucked in a deep breath as I continued. I had to get this out, or I might never have the courage or the opportunity to speak like this again. "Especially after Eve was killed. I didn't know how to handle being a father or being a king without her—and I wasn't sure how the curse worked, or if she really would return. But I should have seen how all of those things were affecting you too. I should have been a better father. I tried to do better with your brothers, but I failed you, and I'm sorry."

He met my gaze properly, and I released a breath at the sudden connection. "Fuck. I've waited thousands of years to hear you say those words."

"I wish I hadn't waited so long to say them." I gave him a wry grin. "Maybe you wouldn't have tried to overthrow me. Twice."

One corner of his mouth curved, the half-smile bitter. "Not some of my finest moments, I'll admit."

"Do you really hate me so much you want me dead?" I asked in a low voice, almost afraid to hear the answer.

He looked down at his hands, wrapping around his drink. "No. I didn't want you dead. I have a lot of regrets. Like siding with Adam and releasing Pestilence. I tried to fix it by becoming War, but we all saw how that turned out."

I didn't speak. This all felt too fragile to disrupt.

"To answer your question, no, I don't hate you," he

continued. "Maybe I did at various times in the past, but not anymore. But I don't regret trying to overthrow you either time. Each time I did it, you'd become out of touch with the people you ruled over, and I knew it was time for a change. No one should rule unchecked for thousands of years. That's the way to despotism. You might not have seen it, but both times the revolution was brewing behind your back even without me. I simply ignited the spark."

I considered his words, and some of the things the Archdemons had said over the last year. Many of them were unhappy that I ended the war with the angels and made us leave Hell, even though I did it to save the demon race. I had no regrets there. Still, perhaps I'd acted too harshly. Perhaps I should have consulted them more. I'd also discovered that many felt Fallen were not truly demons, and that I held my kind above all of the other demonic races. Perhaps I did, as I used them to watch over the other demons and keep them in line. Maybe Belial was right and it was time for a change, though I wasn't giving up my throne so easily.

I stroked my chin as I considered. "Your point is valid. I've started to see that some of that is true, and I'd love to talk with you more about this. Believe it or not, I do not want to become a dictator."

"Yeah, whatever." He shrugged and sipped his drink, back to acting like he didn't give a damn, but I knew better. Like me, he cared—maybe too much, even though he would never admit it. And like me, that was often his downfall. But I was admitting it now.

I raised my glass. "Of course, now that the curse is

broken and your mother is ruling beside me, I have a feeling she'll keep me in line too."

Belial managed to chuckle at that. "No doubt. Not to mention a miniature version of her running around soon."

I groaned. "That's right. It's been so long, I forgot how difficult those early years can be sometimes. I actually think I blocked out the toddler years with all of you. Especially Damien's. What a little monster he was."

Belial actually laughed at that, and we both took a sip of our drinks, settling into a companionable silence. I was having a drink with my son, and all was right in the world.

Belial cleared his throat. "I'll leave Morningstar with you before I go."

I started to open my mouth to accept but I waved my hand instead. "Keep it for now. I want you to be safe, wherever you are."

Morningstar was my angelic sword, forged for me in Heaven back when I'd been an Archangel. When I'd left for Hell and become a Fallen, the sword had changed, allowing it to channel both darkness and light. Only those of my blood could use the sword now, along with Hannah, since she was my mate. It would always come back to me, but for now it felt right with Belial.

He shrugged. "It's not like I plan to use it. I'm heading back to New Orleans. Back to my bar. Back to staying out of this shit."

"I'm not sure that's possible for ones such as us, but I wish you well, and hope to see you again soon." I offered him my hand.

He took it firmly, and we shook hands, meeting each other's eyes. I looked upon my son as an equal, and he looked back at me with something other than hatred and anger.

It was a start.

20

HANNAH

I leaned against Lucifer as we sped along the highway in the limo. We were fresh off his plane and he'd practically whisked me into the car without letting me catch more than a glimpse of a clear blue sky. I hated that he wouldn't tell me where we were going, but he'd said he didn't want to ruin the surprise.

As I gazed out at the freeway we were driving down, my thoughts wandered to my sons, as it often did. I wondered what they were doing now. Belial had gone back to New Orleans to rebuild his bar and try to live a quiet life, Damien had returned to Faerie to spy on Oberon, and Kassiel had gone to upstate New York to teach a class at Hellspawn Academy, the university for demons where I supposed our daughter would go someday. Or would she go to Seraphim Academy, since she was part angel? Hmm.

Lucifer smoothed his hand over my shoulder. "Are you all right?"

I shrugged. "I just miss our sons. I only just found them again and now they're all gone."

Lucifer chuckled but he drew me tighter against him. "It's only been a month since we saw them. A blink of an eye in an immortal lifetime."

"I know." Some days I still felt so very human, even though that had all been a carefully constructed lie.

His hand drifted to my very round stomach. "Soon we'll have another child to look after for many years. We should try to enjoy our last few moments alone together while we can."

"Is that so?" I asked, my voice growing husky. One benefit of being an Elder God—we never ran out of stamina. A good thing too, since these damn pregnancy hormones made me horny all the time.

He pressed a kiss to my neck, as his hands slid back up to palm my breasts. "I like the way you think, my love."

"Do we have time?" I asked, glancing out the window. We were heading toward a freeway exit now.

"Yes, if we make it quick." He raised his head and met my gaze, his wicked green eyes alight with desire. "I have so much I want to show you today."

"I have so much I want to see. How proud are you feeling today, Lucifer?" I grinned at our old joke, but my words came out almost as a low purr.

"Around you, I can barely control my pride."

He pressed his mouth against mine, while I reached for the zipper on his pants, carefully cupping his hard bulge as I did. Sudden desperation for him spurred my movements.

He'd said we should make it quick, after all. Lucifer got the hint and shoved my own pants off, but the stretchy maternity pants made it difficult to do anything with grace or speed.

"What do you desire, darling?" He moved his hand to the top of his pants, unfastened them the rest of the way. Then he freed his cock and palmed it, stroking the hard length.

"I want you, Lucifer."

His rhythm increased as he continued to touch himself. "How do you want me?"

"Here. Now." I was wet for him. So very wet. I watched his fingers moving over his skin, and I whimpered my need.

He gazed upon me with a perfect mix of lust and love. "You've always been my greatest temptation. Every face, every name, every time. Only you."

"Always you, Lucifer." I shoved panties off and moved to sit upon him, facing away, lowering myself onto him before either of us could say another word.

He inhaled sharply and his hands went to my hips, partly to steady me, but almost like he might impose a rhythm. I grabbed his hands and brought them to my breasts instead. He played his long fingers across them, stroking my nipples through the fabric before he started working at my buttons, releasing just enough of them that he could access my skin and dip down beneath my bra.

This wasn't calm and gentle. This was shoving clothes out of the way and grinding on Lucifer to find my pleasure. He swept my hair aside and nibbled my neck, then bit down harder, although not enough to draw pain. Just enough to say he could mark me if he wanted. That I was his. I arched to give him more skin, and he pushed his hips upward, thrusting hard.

I rolled against him, rubbing against the spot that made me cry out. He held on, his hands over my breasts and his mouth at the side of my neck as I lifted up and sank back down. Slow at first, then faster and faster, until the only sounds in the back of the limo were my heavy breaths and the slap of our skin connecting.

"Lucifer." His name left my mouth over and over, like a chant, and it grew faster as I began to lose control. He moved with me, catching hold of my urgency. Finally, my body tightened around him and I sucked in a ragged breath. He pulled me against him and strained upward one last time with his own release. Our orgasms rocked through us, but luckily we'd gotten better at controlling our new powers, and we managed not to destroy the limo we were sitting inside.

"Hannah," he murmured against my ear, before smoothing some of my hair back. He pressed a kiss to the back of my neck as our movements slowed, our lust sated. For now.

The limo stopped, and I glanced out the windows to see a glorious blue sea. I'd been so distracted by Lucifer I'd completely ignored the final part of our journey. Our driver got out of the car and waited patiently for us nearby, giving us time to get dressed. He'd probably heard far too much, even though the privacy screen had been in place. Oh well. We'd give him a big tip at the end of this.

Once dressed, I got out of the car slowly, letting the soft breeze soothe my too-warm cheeks, and inhaled the fresh sea air. "Where are we?"

"Southern California." Lucifer adjusted his suit as he stood beside me. "In fact, we're just a mile away from where Asmodeus and Brandy live now."

"Thank you, Lucifer." I threw my arms around him, and he hugged me close.

"I thought it was time to move forward with our discussion about finding a new home. I wanted you to see this one." He indicated a giant fence with a big gate.

I couldn't help my laugh. "I never in a million years thought I could own a fence as big as that one."

"You can, if you so desire."

The gate opened as if he'd willed it so, and a sweeping driveway lined by palm trees led to a large white house. The grounds of the estate stretched far and wide in every direction, with the sparkling blue ocean behind it.

I paused and looked around at the greens of the trees and the blue of the sea. "This is gorgeous."

"It gets better." Lucifer took my hand as we started along the driveway. The scent of the flowers hung heavy in the hot afternoon air, and I walked slowly to savor them. "You haven't even seen the house yet."

"Forget the house. I think I'd be happy to live outside." I laughed and swung our hands as we walked, freed from my worries by the hope of future happiness.

"Then let's explore the grounds first." Instead of leading me to the front door, we went around the side, where we discovered a large sparkling pool and spa, an outdoor kitchen with a seating area and a cabana, and lots and lots of land, all overlooking the ocean. "There's more than enough room for our horses to roam, and for you to create another garden here."

My mind was already swimming with ideas for what I could design for the space. We continued on, past a guest house that looked bigger than the house I'd lived in with Brandy, and a walkway that led down to a private beach. I stood at the top of it, soaking in the sunshine. Even though I was so much more than an angel now, I still loved it. "It's perfect."

"You like it?" he asked.

I let loose a breath, "I love it."

Lucifer watched my face closely with a small smile. "Let's head inside."

We approached the two-story house, which had an incredible system of miniature waterways running around it between more palm trees. The house boasted wide glass windows and whole walls that seemed to simply fold out of the way to allow the exterior and interior to merge into one luxurious space. My heart beat wildly as I coveted all that I saw. I almost didn't need to see the inside. Lucifer knew me so well after all this time—if this was the house he'd selected to show me, there was no doubt it was the perfect one.

As we stepped through the entrance doorway, I squeezed Lucifer's hand in mine. A big open concept living area flowed into a chef's kitchen and out through a wall of glass doors with access to the vibrant green lawn and turquoise pool, with the ocean glinting in the sun behind it. A glorious staircase led upstairs, while a hallway led off to other rooms to the side. The house was empty of all furniture, but I could already imagine how I would decorate it—lots of black and white, plus sea greens and ocean blues, with a splash of earthy sand tones.

As Lucifer led me further inside, he said, "There's plenty of room for the boys to stay, it's close enough to hop back to Vegas quickly, and it's secluded enough to give us both privacy and safety."

"You don't need to give me a sales pitch," I said with a laugh. "I'm already sold."

Lucifer smirked. "You haven't seen the best part yet."

I lifted an eyebrow. "The bedrooms?"

He shook his head, mock disappointment on his face. "Really? No, love. The library."

I perked up at that. "It has a library?"

A wicked grin lifted his lips. "Of course it does."

We stepped inside, and my mouth fell open. Row after row of white bookshelves lined the big space, which had a view of the ocean behind a spot that looked like the perfect reading nook. It was even bigger than Lucifer's library in Vegas, and I could already imagine all the glorious hours it would take to organize our books in here. Plus, we'd need new ones to fill all these shelves. Naturally. In fact, I was pretty sure I'd need an entire wall to shelve all my favorite romance novels.

There were two guest bedrooms on the first floor, along with an office and a yoga studio we would turn into a sparring room. After we checked them out, we finally headed upstairs. The second floor opened up so you could see the living room below, before leading off into the other bedrooms. The primary bedroom was huge, with an attached room that would be perfect for when the baby was young. The bathroom was just as impressive, all newly remodeled with intriguing 3D tiles that looked like waves, that I just had to run my hand over. The other bedrooms upstairs were also a good size for our daughter to grow up in or for guests when they visited.

"I've seen enough," I said, as I leaned on the handrail on the landing overlooking the first floor. Everything about this home felt right. I could see us raising our daughter here, our horses would have plenty of space, and Brandy was close by. Plus the estate would be easier to defend and more secure than a penthouse in a big city. "Let's make an offer today. I want this house."

"It's yours." Lucifer wrapped his arms around me from behind. "I already bought it."

I spun around in his arms. "You did?"

"The second it came on the market, I made the previous owners an offer they couldn't refuse. I hope you'll forgive me for making the decision on my own, but I wanted to surprise you, and I acted quickly to make sure we didn't lose the property to someone else. It was too perfect to pass up."

"I love it, and I love you for knowing how much I would love it."

"Good." He bent to kiss me, then took my hand and led

me into our future bedroom with a naughty smile playing across his lips. "I think we should celebrate our new home."

"Now?" I asked with a laugh. "We don't even have any furniture yet!"

"I don't need furniture to give you an orgasm." He took me further inside, to the bathroom, and gently set me on the counter. "Besides, if we're going to have sex in every room of this house, we'd better get started."

I shook my head with a rueful smile as he dragged off my pants again, but then his head was between my thighs and his tongue was on my pussy and all I could do was lean back and let him pleasure me. A deep feeling of rightness settled over me, as if destiny had finally led me to this moment after thousands of years of suffering, and now I would have my chance to relax and enjoy my happiness.

I just had to ignore the little voice inside me asking me if it could really last.

21

HANNAH

I wrapped my arms around my beach ball-sized belly and tried to breathe through the contraction tightening through it. It was a week before my due date, and we'd finally managed to move many of our things into our new house in California and bought enough furniture to make it livable. Now all we needed was to set up the nursery. I'd thought we would have another week or longer—all my sons had been born late, but this morning I'd started having contractions. I was sure they were false ones, but it motivated me to get the crib set up immediately—just in case.

"Screwdriver." I held my hand out toward Lucifer as I lifted the headboard of the crib.

"Darling, what exactly are you doing?" He managed to sound both curious and horrified at the same time.

I narrowed my eyes. "This nursery furniture isn't going to put itself together."

"There's an actual man in the room willing to do this for you."

I rolled my eyes. "Okay, actual man. But I think you might need to remember I'm a god now and can do pretty much anything. Even while pregnant."

He took the crib piece off me and set it down before tugging me into his arms and dropping a tender kiss on my lips. "Oh, believe me, I never forget that."

I pressed my palms against his chest. "No distractions. This crib needs to be built right away. We have no idea when this little lady is going to arrive. It could be today, for all we know."

His eyes widened as he glanced down at my belly. "We're not ready yet. Keep her in."

"I'll ask, but I have a feeling she has a mind of her own already." I handed him the screwdriver and sauntered over to the nursing chair. "Now screw like the wind."

He grinned. "Usually when you say that we're both naked."

I chuckled softly and was relieved to be able to sit down for a while. I closed my eyes and rocked myself back and forth on the chair Zel had given me as I rode out another contraction. Shit, they were getting closer, weren't they?

"Where'd Zel get to?" I asked. She'd moved into the guest house as soon as we'd mentioned the new place. No waiting to be invited, no waiting for permission, she just packed a bag to come along with us, then set herself up as head of security for the estate, running it all from the guest house and overseeing a small battalion of guards. I loved Zel, but she could definitely be...intense sometimes. It had only gotten worse after we asked her to be the baby's godmother. Still, if I was going to have this baby today, I wanted her nearby.

"I don't know, but I should order her to help me with this crib. She's a lot more handy than I am." Lucifer looked to the door like he might actually run down to the guesthouse and fetch her.

Despite Lucifer's complaints, he continued to get the crib set up, while I rested and gazed across the nursery. Over the last few days I'd decorated it like a secret garden, with little floral touches everywhere. The room made me happy and calm, and I hoped our daughter liked it too.

"Knock knock," Samael said, and I looked up at the unexpected voice at the doorway.

"So much for increased security," Lucifer grumbled. "Looks like Zel's letting in any old riff-raff these days."

I beckoned Samael in with a smile. "Perfect timing. You can help Lucifer look like he knows what he's doing with that crib."

Lucifer shook the screwdriver at me. "I beg your pardon, but I've finished the crib, thank you very much. Although now I need to mount this changing table to the wall. Can't have it tipping over in an earthquake."

I shook my head. "How humbling that even though we are gods we still have to worry about things like earthquakes."

"Have you come with an update?" Lucifer asked Samael, as he began attaching the mounting straps to the wall. Samael had been running things from Vegas ever since we moved out here, allowing us to step back from demon matters so we could focus on the new house and the baby.

"I have." Samael gave a small bow, but I noticed he didn't step forward to help Lucifer with his task. "The imps have been leaderless ever since Hannah killed Nemesis. They haven't chosen a new Archdemon yet and are fighting amongst themselves for control."

Lucifer grinned. "Why am I not surprised? At least that should keep them out of our hair for a while."

"Indeed."

"And the shifters?" I asked my question as I rode out another contraction in my rocking chair. This one was stronger, and I had to grip the armrests through it. "Have we found Fenrir?"

Samael cast an inquisitive look at me, as though he'd noticed I wasn't well, but was too polite to say anything. "No, I'm sorry to say he hasn't been seen. We believe he and the other shifters loyal to him are in hiding for the time being, no doubt plotting their next moves."

"I'm sure they're trying to figure out a way to release Death even now," Lucifer said.

"Would they really be that foolish?" I asked. "Surely they can see there's no way they can win at this point."

Lucifer leaned against the wall as he took a break from his work. "Fenrir is stubborn, and long ago an Erelim angel had all these prophecies about Ragnarok that he believed. He probably thinks releasing Death will set that off."

I thought back to everything I knew about Norse mythology. "Isn't he meant to die in Ragnarok though?"

Samael sniffed. "In the ancient days, every Erelim angel had their own prophecy about the apocalypse, and most of them contradicted each other. Some of these prophecies we've already stopped from coming true over the years. Like that 2012 Mayan Apocalypse."

Lucifer groaned. "Don't remind me. What a pain that was."

"What are you talking about?" I asked.

"A portal to Void was meant to open on the day the Mayan calendar ended in Tikal in Guatemala," Samael explained. "It could have released dozens of Elder Gods, but we managed to shut it down before anything happened."

"Just like we're going to stop the Four Horsemen's apocalypse before it happens too," Lucifer said.

Samael nodded. "Pestilence's tomb still holds, and Theo and his gargoyles are guarding it. They'll report any changes to me immediately."

I prayed Pestilence stayed locked up for a very long time. I wanted my baby to grow up without the threat of Adam casting a shadow over her childhood. He'd already done so much harm to our family—all I wanted was to not have to worry about him coming after us again.

Samael lapsed into silence, but something about the conversation felt unfinished. Lucifer glanced up like he felt it too.

"Is everything else okay?" I asked. Samael was Lucifer's greatest friend and ally, and we both owed him a lot. If he was unhappy with the current situation, we would fix it however we could.

"Yes." At first I thought Samael wasn't going to say anything further, then he cleared his throat and looked away. "I took your advice, Lucifer. On the way here, I stopped to see Asmodeus and his new family."

"Really?" I leaned forward, so excited by this unexpected turn of events I barely noticed the contraction. Okay, that was a lie, it hurt like hell.

Samael had been so upset by his son Asmodeus turning mortal that he'd refused to have anything to do with him for the last few months. Lucifer and I had begged him to give his son a chance, to meet Brandy, to forgive Lilith for making their son mortal. All we wanted was for him to talk to his son, if nothing else. Especially now that Brandy was pregnant too.

"How did it go?" Lucifer asked, as he gave Samael his full attention. He knew all about reconnecting with estranged sons, and how challenging it could be.

"It went well. I've come to accept my son's decision, even though it pains me. I can see he is truly in love, and has found a family that makes him happy." He hesitated. "I'd had no idea my son wanted something like that. I thought he was happy as an incubus, but now I realize how miserable he'd been. I just never expected him to end up with a human."

"Brandy is his mate," I said, feeling defensive of my best friend. "And she's a good person. She took care of me when I had no idea who I was, and accepted me when I told her I was an angel dating Lucifer."

Samael inclined his head. "I have nothing but respect for the woman who managed to tame my son."

"And Lilith?" Lucifer asked. "Have you spoken with her?"

Samael scowled a little at that. "No. Not yet."

Lucifer rested a hand on his friend's shoulder. "If there's anything I've learned from all of this, it's that family is everything. They say time heals all wounds, but maybe this one could use a little help."

Samael's lips pressed into a tight line, but then he said, "Fine, I will make an effort to speak with Lilith, even if only to stop this infernal flirting she does in front of Baal."

"About damn time," Lucifer said.

Another contraction shook through me, and this one was followed by a feeling like I'd peed myself. I'd had enough babies to know that meant my water had broken.

"It's also time over here," I said, unable to deny it any longer. "Send for Marcus. The baby is coming."

Lucifer dropped the screwdriver. "Now?"

I nodded. "Now."

22

LUCIFER

Hannah grimaced more than smiled and she gripped the hand I'd offered her with all the strength of a god. Good thing I was one too, or she'd have broken me.

"That's it. Keep breathing." I'd intended to be soothing, but she shot me a glare and I closed my mouth, relegated to be the hand she was holding. Marcus waited at the foot of the bed, but I was under strict instructions to stay by her head and leave the business end to someone else, which suited me just fine.

It had been a long labor, and even though Hannah had borne three children before, she hadn't done it in this body, which made everything different. Equal parts anticipation and sadness floated through my mind as Marcus told her to push. Meeting a daughter for the first time would be a wondrous thing, especially after our last one had been taken from us too soon, but I was also keenly aware this would be the last time I ever experienced this.

And while that burden was mostly Hannah's, she'd sacrificed herself for me and that responsibility weighed heavily.

But I couldn't afford to think of that now. Not while my mate needed me. Besides, the excitement outweighed the sadness. Today we would complete our family.

I tried to listen while Marcus coached Hannah through the birth process, but my attention was all on my mate, holding her hand through every breath she gasped. I knew the pain of this moment would fade, as it had with each of the boys, and we'd be left with a miracle.

My love for Hannah grew as I watched her amazing body bring forth the life we'd created together. Even this was a sacrifice of sorts—volunteering her body for our love. I'd lived thousands of years and seen many amazing things in that time, but this was the most incredible and unbelievable, the way life continued.

"One more push!" Marcus's voice was calm and soothing, and he was probably easing Hannah's pain as he guided our daughter into the world. Still, I saw her tense up and it made my protective side come out.

"Are you sure you've done this before?" I asked Marcus. I knew he was a great healer, Archangel Raphael's son even, but did he really know how to deliver a baby?

Marcus rolled his eyes and ignored me. I scowled and considered threatening him and everyone he loved if he didn't get this baby out immediately, but then Hannah's eyes met mine and I forced myself to be calm. Deep breaths. I swept Hannah's hair away from her forehead and let her grip my hand. I couldn't do anything else but be with her. In this role, being the Demon King was essentially useless.

Suddenly Hannah let out a guttural roar and a wave of power released from her. A heavy gust of air rushed through the room, sending medical supplies flying. Light and darkness burst out of Hannah all at once, and bright green plants suddenly grew up around us, before immediately withering and dying. Through it all, Hannah drained the life of everyone around us as she cried out, and though my powers as War protected me from the brunt of it, I saw Marcus stagger and grip the edge of the bed, his body weak.

"Hannah!" I cupped her chin, forcing her to look at me. "You must control your powers!"

She blinked at me and then the soul-sucking feeling of her draining our life force died off. She drew in a deep breath as she regained control of herself. "Sorry!"

I pressed a kiss to her forehead as she relaxed a little and the room returned to normal. Marcus recovered quickly and got back to work, and soon a thin cry pierced the air as our daughter was brought into the world. Hannah's eyes widened as the baby girl was placed on her bare chest, allowing her to connect immediately with this beautiful, wrinkled, sticky creature that was our baby. I wedged myself onto a thin sliver of bed beside Hannah, wrapping an arm around her as I gazed upon both of them with love.

While Marcus healed Hannah up, she cradled our daughter, and I cradled her, stroking her hair. No words were needed as we shared a moment of quiet, calm love.

"Take the baby, Lucifer," she eventually murmured.

Suddenly I was accepting our daughter into my arms, and I held her against my chest and smiled down at her. She seemed to look at me with recognition, and a small pink arm waved from inside her blanket as I settled her in the crook of my arm.

"Perfect." The word came out as a whisper, and I barely saw Hannah's smile widen before I refocused all of my attention on the child in my arms. I stroked her cheek with the very tip of my finger, careful of the new, fragile skin. "Just beautiful."

Love surged through me, and my chest tightened. The sound that came from my mouth could have been the start of a laugh or a choked sob, and I didn't care if neither was the expected reaction from the Demon King on the birth of his only daughter.

I kissed the baby's little red face and reached for Hannah's hand. My amazing mate had done it again. I was truly the luckiest immortal in the world.

"What are you going to call her?" Marcus asked.

"Funny enough, we haven't discussed that." I perched on the first chair I found and gazed at my daughter's little face, her beautiful blue eyes, and I offered my finger for her to grasp. I glanced at Hannah, and she smiled as she moved her gaze from me to our daughter and back again.

"How about Aurora?" she asked softly. "After your mother."

My chest tightened as I looked into my daughter's eyes again, the color of the sky at dawn. "Yes, that's perfect."

"I'll let you come up with the middle name," Hannah

said, as she leaned back and closed her eyes, no doubt exhausted from everything her body had just gone through.

I considered various names for some time. Since Hannah has chosen to honor a member of my family, I thought it only fitting we do the same for her. "How would you feel about Jophiel?"

Tears gleamed in Hannah's eyes as she smiled at me. "I think Jo would approve."

Marcus and his assistant—who I'd barely even noticed was here this whole time—finished cleaning up, and left us alone for some privacy, saying they would return to check on us shortly. I handed the baby back to Hannah, and she began attempting to breastfeed.

"She's powerful," I said quietly, as I watched them. "I can feel it, even here. The perfect blend of both of us."

"With a little bit of Elder God thrown in for good measure," Hannah said with a laugh.

"Do you think Famine changed her?" I asked.

"No, not at all. But my becoming Famine changed Aurora too, since we were still connected." Hannah sighed a little. "Famine said she wanted to be a mother again, and I sensed she would never hurt this baby. If anything, she made sure Aurora was protected during the transition. I had no love for Famine, but I appreciated that."

I smoothed a hand over my daughter's fuzzy head. No one like her had ever been brought into existence before. Half angel, half Fallen, with a touch of Elder God. I already knew she would be destined for greatness. Of course, we first had to get through the toddler years. Or worse, the teenage years. Somehow I had a feeling she wouldn't make them easy on us. She was a fighter, like her mother.

Our daughter had the power to destroy the world—or end it. I only hoped we were up to the challenge of being her parents.

23

HANNAH

The next few months passed in a sleepless, newborn haze, although Aurora didn't suffer from lack of attention. Our closest friends came to visit regularly, and Zel took her godmother duties far too seriously, proving the intensity we'd predicted from her was right on the money. She'd already tried to give Aurora two tiny knives like her own, and I'd had to explain that it would be a few years at least until my daughter would be ready for combat training.

Despite being an Elder God and not needing sleep, I was somehow exhausted most of the time, and it was a relief when Lucifer suggested I go out and finally take my horse for a ride. We'd made a small stable for the horses on one side of our estate along with a big grazing area, and even though the horses didn't really need any tending to, they seemed to enjoy having a space of their own.

I went out there now, breathing in the glorious fresh air, and found both horses together in the grass. Misery immediately came over to me and nuzzled me with her nose, and I smiled. I'd been so busy I hadn't made much time to get to know her, and I was excited to go for a ride and have a little me time, something that was rare as a new mother.

I climbed onto her back with ease, my body somehow knowing what to do even though I hadn't ridden a horse in centuries. I wove my fingers in her thick black mane, and then she took off with a triumphant leap, racing down the grass. Strife just shook his head and stayed behind as we galloped around the estate, and then we trotted down the rocky path to the beach. Once on the sand, Misery took off at top speed, and I threw my arms out and laughed as the sunshine filled me with life.

Riding across the beach gave me a lot of time to be alone with my thoughts without a baby demanding my attention. I wondered how my sons were doing, and hoped they would visit us soon, but I knew they were all busy with their own lives too. I thought about Samael running things from Vegas, and how nice it was to have some time to step back from all of that. I loved being the Demon Queen, but I also loved being Aurora's mother. My thoughts then turned to Lucifer, who seemed to enjoy being a father again too. The only thing that bothered me was that we hadn't been very intimate since Aurora was born. Hell, we'd barely had a moment alone together since then. I knew that was normal though—after all we'd been through this three times before —but thanks to Marcus and my Elder God healing my body had long been ready. It was more a matter of finding time and energy with a newborn. I just hoped that having a baby

—a baby we both knew would be the last—wasn't going to change our relationship. Each experience seemed more important and immediate when we knew it was the last time we'd ever go through these moments, and I wanted to sear them all into my memories forever.

I wasn't sure how long I rode up and down the California coast, but eventually it was time to return to the stable. As I slid off Misery's back, I felt our connection strongly, this horse that was mine and yet also free. A part of her soul was bound to mine through some ancient magic I didn't understand, but I welcomed her calm, steady presence.

"I'll ride you again soon," I promised, as I patted her back. "And you still need a new name. How about...Shadow?"

A soft neigh signaled to me that she liked that name, and it was settled. It seemed fitting somehow, since I was an angel that lived between light and darkness. Shadow wandered off to stand with Strife, the two of them content in their new home. Like this, they certainly didn't look like horses of the apocalypse. I wondered if Lucifer would rename his horse too. We were still Famine and War, but we kept those dark parts of ourselves in check using everything else we were. We'd figured out how to control our powers...and our cravings. Sometimes I did still get an urge to drain all the life out of every plant around me, but like someone battling an addiction, I worked through it and overcame it.

I checked the time—nap time. One of my favorite times

of day, especially when I looked down at Aurora's sleeping form. Tiny eyelashes against delicate cheeks, a cherubic mouth, a face so peaceful and innocent it seemed unreal. Sometimes I watched her for hours, almost unable to breathe past the love constricting my chest. How could I have forgotten it felt like this?

I strolled into Aurora's nursery, preparing to get everything ready for her nap, nearly tripping over the millions of toys and baby products. I'd had three kids before Aurora, but I'd never had so much *stuff* before. Some of it did certainly make things easier though. I'd have killed for one of those automatic rockers when Belial was a baby—that boy had been the worst sleeper ever. Modern women had no idea how easy they had it compared to the olden days.

Inside the nursery I found the light already dimmed, the blackout curtains tightly closed, and a shirtless, muscular man standing near the crib. Lucifer turned toward me and held a finger to his lips, as he cradled our sleeping daughter against his chest. I smiled back, feeling a burst of love at the sight of them together like this. Lucifer and I had been through so much over the centuries, both together and apart, especially over these last few years—but it was all worth it for moments like these.

Also, Lucifer half-naked and holding our baby? Seriously hot. My mouth practically watered at the sight. Then he bent over to put Aurora in her crib, giving me a view of his perfect ass, and I nearly fanned myself. Who would have thought that the devil could be such a good dad?

We stepped outside and closed the door, and Lucifer asked, "Did you have a nice ride?"

"It was great. I really needed some alone time. Thanks for watching Aurora."

"Of course. We had a lovely day, although it took a bit of rocking to get her to sleep. I forgot how hard all this newborn stuff is. You'd think after three other kids it would get easier somehow..."

"I know." I took his hand and tugged him toward our room. "In fact, I was just thinking maybe we should have some alone time too."

He arched an eyebrow. "Is that so?"

As soon as Lucifer entered the bedroom, I shoved him against the wall and plastered myself against him, my hands smoothing over his shoulders as I lifted myself on my tiptoes for a kiss. He only hesitated for a fraction of a second before his arms wrapped around my waist and he held me tight against him. He spun us around so I had my back against the wall, and his tongue slipped between my lips as he deepened our kiss.

"Hello there," he murmured against my lips as heat shot to my clit. "Is someone feeling a bit randy today?"

I ran my hands along his sculpted abs. "Like you didn't do this on purpose, walking around all half-naked like that."

He donned an innocent expression. "It's hot today."

"You're right, it is hot. I should take off my clothes too." I grabbed my shirt and pulled it over my head.

His eyes raked over my exposed skin. "Probably a good

idea. In fact, we should both take a nice refreshing shower to cool off, don't you think?"

"It has been some time since I showered," I admitted with a laugh. Mom life didn't leave much room for showers at the moment.

"Time to get you cleaned up." He picked me up and carried me into the bathroom, then set me down while he turned on the shower. It was big enough to house five people at least, with water spraying from multiple directions, plus the perfect little bench.

Our clothes were quickly shed, and then we stepped aside into the hot water, behind the steamed-up glass walls. As I stepped under the spray, I pressed my naked breasts against Lucifer's bare chest. He dropped his head, his mouth hot and urgent against my neck, his tongue against my collarbone, and I whimpered when pure need flooded me. I ground against him, relishing the hard length of his cock pushing against my skin as he rolled his hips. I could feel all of him against me, melting me, turning me molten under his touch.

As the water sprayed on us, Lucifer drew his fingertips across my breasts, and my nipples hardened instantly. His hair looked black while wet, and his gaze burned with darkness and the promise of pleasure to come. His mouth crashed against mine again, his hands in my wet hair, his body wrapping around mine. I could barely breathe. But really, who needed to breathe. I had Lucifer, who moved between kissing my mouth, my face, my shoulders and however much lower he could reach.

He groaned and lifted me, his hands supporting my ass as I wrapped my legs over his hips. His mouth trailed heat all over my skin, and I pushed my hands into his hair to hold him closer. His cock nudged against my slippery wet skin and he hissed out a breath.

"Lucifer." His name was little more than a strangled sound on my lips, and he responded straight away, pressing the tip of himself inside me before I even knew he was there. "More."

His mouth was a tight line of control as he eased more of his length into me. I stretched around him, and he groaned. "Fuck, I needed this," he growled as he began to rock into me. "I needed you."

"Then take me," I said, my legs tightening around him. "Take everything."

My back hit the cool tile, and Lucifer put his hands on either side of my head as his cock plunged deep inside me. He moved with the speed and strength of a god, fucking me so hard I was surprised the tile didn't crack, but then he paused, his breathing ragged, like he'd only just realized what he was doing.

"You won't break me," I said, and some of the tension in his muscles disappeared. "I'm a god too. I can handle it."

He pumped into me harder and faster, making me cry out in a mix of pleasure and pain. I was the only one who he could fuck like this, with complete abandon and all of his strength, and the knowledge he would never hurt me. He brought us both to the kind of orgasm you shouted through, the kind that made you forget your name or where you were, the kind that made your body ache in a good way for days.

But he wasn't done yet.

Abruptly, Lucifer held me closer and stepped out of the shower, dripping wet. He walked out onto the balcony, setting me down on the low edge of it, as the soft breeze tickled our water-coated skin. Then he dropped one hand between us, using his finger to stroke over my clit, even as his cock remained hard inside me. He leaned over me, his hips moving slowly, his finger lazy over me, his lips suddenly at my nipple, his tongue drawing it into a fresh peak. I briefly wondered if any of our staff was watching us, but then all thought was gone as his fingers pinched my clit and his teeth brushed against my breasts.

"Don't stop." I clutched his upper arms as I watched his shoulders flex and move like he was made of pure muscle. Lucifer was so hard and strong inside and around me still, even after that first incredible orgasm. He thrust into me faster, his movements so familiar yet still exciting, and I gasped as he took hold of my hips, raising me to adjust his angle. With the afternoon sun shining down on us and the ocean at my back, I threw back my head and lost myself in the moment.

My lips parted as I sucked in a breath and every muscle tensed inside me as pleasure rushed to my core. His eyes widened as my pussy gripped him tight, and then his seed spilled inside me for a second time. Together we hung in a moment of ultimate pleasure, as if our power had managed to stop time. For all I knew, maybe it did. It wouldn't be the strangest thing I'd seen.

"Hannah," he murmured between kisses, and though it was only my name, it said everything I needed to hear. It told me that he still loved me as much as he always had. It told me that even though we'd had a baby, our relationship with each other hadn't changed. It told me that our love was eternal.

Then the baby cried out, and we both sighed, pressing our foreheads together with a little laugh. Time to get back to work.

24

HANNAH

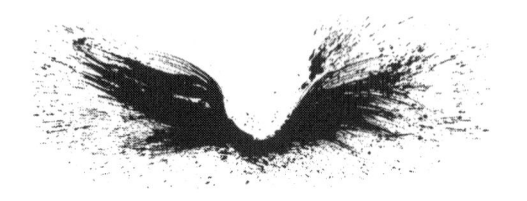

I scanned the gardens with a smile, watching our guests mingle under the pastel pink and yellow tents. Everyone was here, and my heart danced a happy beat seeing all the people I loved grab champagne and little pastries to celebrate Aurora's birth. Soft music played in the background, and the cool sea breeze kept the air from getting too hot, even under the bright afternoon sun. It was a perfect day for a party.

Before angels and demons moved to Earth, having a baby was so rare and special that it was common to have a big celebration so that others could come and pay their respects. Now that our two races lived on Earth, our fertility had increased and these parties were not as common. We decided to have one anyway, mainly as an excuse to get everyone together in one place, and because Lucifer seemed to want a party. I could take the guy out of Vegas but I couldn't take the Vegas out of the guy.

Lucifer wrapped his arm around me, appearing as I thought of him—as he often did. "What are you thinking about?"

I turned and kissed him, a fleeting brush across his lips. "Just how much you must miss your life in Vegas."

He glanced at the sleeping baby in my arms. "I don't miss it at all. This moment in time is so fleeting. I want to spend every second with my daughter while I can."

I knew exactly how he felt. Something like sorrow tightened my chest as I watched Aurora, her chubby hand a fist by her face as she slept. Each of these moments was my actual last. Last baby cries, last night wakings, last set of firsts—sitting up, crawling, walking, talking. Even so, I had no regrets at all. I'd saved our family, and knowing Aurora was our last child only made me appreciate every second with her even more.

And today was a day to celebrate her.

Lilith walked down the path toward us, dressed in a short sundress that was both sexy and cute, and I smiled as I saw her. Baal and Gabriel accompanied her, and it never ceased to amaze me that she'd managed to coax both an Archdemon and an Archangel into sharing her. I was glad she was back with them though, especially since she had a daughter with each one.

Then I nearly fell over with shock when Samael appeared and took her hand, then leaned close and gave her a quick kiss. A real kiss too, not just some polite cheek kiss. Were they together now too?

"Did you know?" I asked Lucifer, trying to keep my

smile in place, even though my eyes were surely bulging out of their sockets at this unexpected surprise.

Lucifer donned a huge grin. "I guess Samael did a lot more than just talk to Lilith."

It was about time they'd gotten together. Lilith had been flirting hardcore with Samael for a while now, and it was obvious to everyone that Samael still had feelings for her, even though he'd done everything he could to resist her. Obviously he'd finally succumbed to her many charms, and gotten over whatever issues they'd had. Perhaps there was just no resisting a force of nature such as Lilith.

"Well, well," Lucifer said as the four of them arrived within conversation distance. His eyes danced with amusement and he wore a self-satisfied smirk. "Fancy seeing the four of you together."

"You all look great," I said, although that was probably no better a phrase to lead with. "It's really wonderful to see you all...getting along so well."

Lilith chuckled, deep and throaty. "Thank you. We're so happy to be here."

Baal rolled his eyes, while Gabriel just shrugged. Samael looked embarrassed by it all and said, "It's all very new, of course."

"Now you need one more to complete your set," Lucifer told Lilith. "What about that fae lord you used to be involved with?"

Lilith's eyes flared, a small smile capturing her lips. "Never say never."

Gabriel clasped his hand on Lucifer's shoulder. "Glad to

see you're back to yourself again, old friend, and congratulations on the new baby."

"Thank you." Lucifer glanced over at Olivia, who stood with Callan, Marcus, Bastien, and Kassiel as they talked to Raphael and a few other angels. "You sure you don't want another one yourself?"

Gabriel let out a hearty laugh. "I think two are enough for me right now. Although I wouldn't mind a grandkid. Those seem like all the fun with none of the responsibility."

"Grandkids are wonderful," Baal said with a nod. Long ago he'd had numerous children with different women, forming an entire line stretching back thousands of years, known as The House of Baal. Of course, he also had a teenage daughter with Lilith named Lena, who was only now coming into her demon powers. It still remained to be seen whether she would be a vampire or a succubus—demons could only be one type, and it emerged when they were eighteen.

"Yes, they are," Samael said. He donned a rare smile, his eyes landing on Asmodeus and Brandy, who was holding their newborn son, born a month after my own. "I look forward to getting to know mine."

"May I hold her?" Lilith asked.

"Of course." I started to pass Aurora to Lilith, but then Zel popped up.

"Careful!" Zel said, making Lilith jump.

"I assure you, I know what I'm doing," Lilith drawled. "I've had many more children than you, my dear."

"Zel takes her godmotherly duties very seriously." I

waved at Zel to back off. I often wondered if someone told Zel that godmother meant twenty-four-hour bodyguard. I loved Zel, but sometimes it was a bit much.

"Just looking out for my girl," Zel muttered, before slinking away with a scowl.

Samael came to stand at Lilith's elbow, and Lilith and her mates all gazed down at my sleeping baby. Baal stroked her head softly, and Gabriel touched her little hand. It struck me then that years ago, none of this could have happened—angels and demons celebrating the birth of one that shared both their blood.

"She's gorgeous," Lilith said, as she handed Aurora back to me. "Thank you for letting me hold her."

She headed off to speak with Romana, who stood with Theo and some other gargoyles. Her entourage followed behind her, and I could barely hold in a giggle at the sight of all of them, even stoic Samael, acting like puppies at her heel.

Lucifer wrapped an arm around me and drew me close. "Did you ever think we could pull this off?"

"Hmm?" I half turned to him, enjoying the faint scratch of his cheek against mine.

He waved in the general direction of our guests. "Angels and demons at a party together, honoring a child born of both races."

I shook my head with a smile. "I was just thinking the same thing."

When Lucifer had first found me as Hannah, this sort of thing had been impossible to even consider. Angels and demons had been at war, and we'd had to hide our relationship for fear of what would happen if anyone found out that the devil was in love with the daughter of an Archangel. Now such pairings were becoming more and more normal.

"It's all thanks to you," I said, pressing a kiss to his cheek. "You brought peace to our people. It was no wonder you were able to defeat War. You're the opposite of him in every way."

"Just as you're the opposite of Famine." He lifted a shoulder in a casual shrug. "But I only did it out of love for you and hope for a future where we could be together."

"Now we're living in that future." He and I would do everything in our power to keep this peace too, especially now that we had Aurora. Years ago, she would have been forbidden. An abomination. Some might have even called for her death. Now she would live in both the angel and demon worlds, like me, and I hoped she would be embraced by each side.

Suddenly the sky darkened as large wings covered the sun. Three dragons flew overhead, circling down to us, and everyone went on alert. Weapons were drawn, wings expanded, and claws came out. Lucifer and I were ready to unleash the Elder Gods inside us, if needed. But then the dragons set down calmly on the beach, shifted into their human forms, and began walking toward us with no obvious hostility. The man in front was tall and muscular with short black hair and a sharp jaw, and though I'd only seen him in his dragon form, I knew this was Valefar, their leader.

"We come to pledge the dragons' loyalty to the Demon

King and Queen," Valefar said, as he dropped into a bow before us, his fist over his heart. The man and woman behind him did the same. "And to pay our respects to the little princess."

We'd long been hoping the dragons would finally join us again, but I'd never expected them to show up today like this. Lucifer had one hand on me, gripping me tight as I held Aurora protectively, and he glanced at me with one eyebrow raised. Silently asking me if Valefar spoke the truth. Though Valefar's words had all been honest, I checked his aura anyway, and saw no deception or malice there. I gave Lucifer a subtle nod in return, and he let me go and took a step closer to Valefar.

"Welcome, Archdemon Valefar," Lucifer said. "We're pleased you could join us, and we accept your loyalty oath."

Valefar rose up and gestured at his companions, who each offered a small, wrapped present. "We've brought gifts for your daughter."

"That's very kind of you," I said, as Lucifer took the gifts. "Please enjoy the party and make yourselves comfortable."

"Yes, later we can discuss how best to return the dragons to the fold," Lucifer said. "For now, grab some champagne."

"Thank you." Valefar and his companions gave us another bow, and then they headed for the bar. Romana walked over and began talking to him while the bartender poured him a drink, and it was clear the two of them knew each other already. Perhaps she'd convinced him to side with us.

That only left the imps and shifters unaccounted for,

but the imps still had no Archdemon to lead them, and no one had seen Fenrir since he'd leaped through the portal out of Faerie. Even the other shifters we'd spoken to, some of whom still sided with Lucifer, had no clue what he was up to at the moment.

Suddenly a portal opened up on the other side of the garden, startling all the people at the party, who had just gone back to talking after the last surprising arrival. But now the fae were here, and they always liked to make an entrance.

Damien stepped through first, followed by my mother, who looked radiant in a pale yellow gown with real daisies growing out of it. Fae fashion could be a bit...extreme. Damien was much more subdued in a simple white silk shirt and black trousers, and he took his grandmother by the elbow and led her toward us. Lucifer tensed beside me at the sight of Demeter, though he stepped forward to give his son a hug.

"It's good to see you again, Damien." Then he shot a hard look at my mother. "Demeter."

"Lucifer." Her voice was frosty, and her gaze equally cool as it moved from my mate to me. "Hannah."

I ignored her as I hugged my son, then handed him the baby so he could meet her properly. Aurora's eyes popped open and she giggled and cooed at her brother, who laughed with her.

"You've already decided I'm your favorite brother, haven't you?" Damien asked, as she grabbed his finger. "Oh yes, she's a clever one."

I turned toward Demeter and offered her a smile. "Thanks for coming, Mother. Would you like to meet your granddaughter?"

My mother's face immediately changed, losing all hint of frostiness, lighting up as if from within, becoming truly beautiful the way only a fae could. She held her arms out to Damien, and as soon as she held Aurora against her, she touched the baby's face gently with a smile. Then she reached out a hand to me, and I took it. How could I not? She was my mother, the only one still alive from all my previous lives. I knew this hadn't been easy for her—to lose a daughter who was then replaced by a stranger, more than once. I looked at Aurora and couldn't even imagine.

My mother's fierce protectiveness of the daughter she'd loved reminded me of Jophiel and her desire to pause me as Hannah so she wouldn't lose me. Demeter clung to her grief over Persephone in the same way. Though I didn't agree with their actions, I knew they did them out of love, and I tried not to judge them too harshly. I'd lost my chance to reconcile with my sister, but maybe I still had a chance with my mother. Even if she was only here because of my daughter, it was a start.

After my mother had finally released Aurora, and Zel had stopped hanging around like some kind of armed hellhound, Lucifer and I sat with our children around the fire pit as it burned to embers and the sky darkened. Guests had drifted away or left the party entirely, and the only ones still left were family. Even Belial was with us. All of our children, gathered in one place, for the first time—but hopefully not the last.

Kassiel held Aurora and smiled down at her as he rocked her to sleep. She was perfectly content and happy there, but then he passed her to Damien and she began to cry immediately.

"Thought you were good with women, Damien." Kassiel smirked at his brother, and Damien briefly covered his sister's eyes to flip his younger brother off.

"Only ones that aren't my sister." Damien turned his attention to Aurora, and she soon giggled at the expressions he made, her gaze tracking every movement of his face. "Besides, we can't all be the perfect brother."

Kassiel shrugged as he leaned back and took a sip of his beer. "I'm just happy I'm not the baby in the family anymore."

"You're always going to be the baby brother, Kass," Belial said with a grin. "I still remember changing your diapers and rocking you to sleep."

Damien offered the baby to Belial. "Show us how it's done then, old man."

Belial snorted. "She seems happy where she is."

"Oh no, I insist."

Despite his boastful words, our eldest son looked uncomfortable as he awkwardly took the baby into his tattooed arms. I snuggled against Lucifer, content to watch my sons pass their sister between them, and curious to see what would happen next.

Belial's hard expression softened as he looked down at his sister. She stopped yawning and reached for his face, touching his lips, and clubbing his chin with her little closed fist. He grinned and caught her hand, and she moved her mouth like she had something to say. He said something softly to her that was only for her ears, and then she settled down and closed her eyes. Within a few seconds, she was asleep.

Belial leaned back in his chair and gave us a cocky grin. "See? Still got the touch."

"Maybe you just bored her to sleep," Damien said. "I heard it's a common problem with your women."

"What women?" Kassiel asked with a snort. "Hasn't Belial been celibate since the 1600s?"

Belial rolled his eyes. "Don't make me come over there and kick both your asses. I could do it without even waking her up, you know."

Lucifer chuckled softly. "As amusing as that would be to watch, there will be no fighting tonight. Don't upset your poor mother."

"I'm just glad you got her to sleep," I said, amused by their banter. It had been so long since we'd all hung out together like this, and I wasn't sure when it would happen again. I just wanted to sit here and soak up this moment for as long as I could. After all, none of us knew when another threat would emerge and put us all in danger again. It was inevitable, being who we were, and all we could do was try to enjoy the peace while it lasted.

25

HANNAH

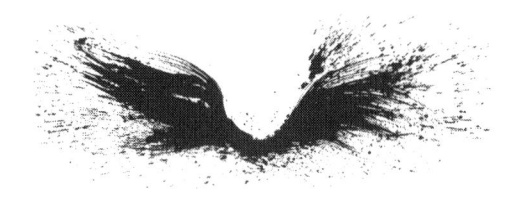

Time passed, and still no threat had emerged. I was starting to think my idyllic life might actually be the new norm. How was that possible? I didn't know, but I wasn't going to question it, not after living hundreds of tormented lives where I was brutally torn apart from everyone I loved. Maybe the universe had finally decided I should get a reprieve.

I sipped my coffee as I looked at the two babies lying on a mat in front of me. There was only a month between them, but while Brandy's son Isaac was content to sit on his butt and survey the world from the cushions that propped him in place, Aurora already seemed desperate to move and get going, rolling to things that interested her and attempting to inch across our hardwood floors like a worm. Occasionally, she got close enough to Isaac to take one of his toys, and that was the most animated he became—his voice loud until

Brandy soothed his little hurt feelings with a replacement block.

We had baby playdates like this every week, and it was fun seeing our kids grow up together. I just loved living so close to Brandy, since it reminded me of when we were roommates and would hang out all the time. It was also nice to be around someone who was human, who treated me as an equal and not a queen, who reminded me of what it was like to be mortal.

Brandy handed her son another block to gnaw on and gazed at him with adoration lighting her eyes. "Six months and all he wants to do is chew on things."

"That's what babies do," I said with a laugh. "I'm pretty sure Aurora is getting her first tooth. She's been so fussy lately."

Aurora reached into the air like she could see something besides dust motes in the sunlight filtering through the open windows. The smell of the Pacific drifted in off a gentle breeze, and palm trees rustled and rattled together in our gardens. I leaned back against a cushion and curled my legs under me, content with this new calm, normal existence.

"How's Lucifer doing, being so far away from his empire?" Brandy's lips formed a mischievous smile.

"He doesn't seem to mind. Besides, he can run pretty much everything from his office here, and Samael takes care of the rest." Brandy didn't need to know too much about demon business, no matter how much I loved my friend. Her life was much more simple, even though she was married to a former incubus. Besides, she was safer if she didn't know everything. "How's Asmodeus?"

"He's good, although he's super bored now that he doesn't have a job running Lucifer's strip clubs for all the Lilim. He's been joking he's going to open up a male version of Hooters called Peckers and fill it with incubus servers."

I nearly spit out my coffee as I laughed. "That would be hilarious."

"Yep. I think he might be serious too. He says succubi get all the attention, and he wants to provide more opportunities for incubi to get fed without hurting humans."

It was just like Asmodeus to still be watching over his fellow demons even though he was now mortal and removed from our world. "Then he should do it. I'm sure Lucifer would support it."

"Maybe. I told him he should just open some little cafes along the coast, but he said that wasn't sexy enough." She laughed and shook her head. "Once a sex demon, always a sex demon, I suppose."

I shrugged. "We can't change our true nature, even if we're made mortal."

Brandy was about to reply when her eyes widened. My head jerked back to Aurora, who wasn't on the floor beside Isaac anymore, but in the air, making unsteady progress as she chased a seed that had blown in on the breeze. Two wings had emerged from her back, one pure black and trailing darkness from it, the other as white as fresh snow and glowing brightly. They fluttered uncertainly, barely keeping her airborne as she made her way clumsily toward the window that held her fascination.

I launched myself to my feet, my breath stuck in my chest, my mug clattering to the floor and spilling coffee everywhere. "Aurora! No!"

I caught her in my arms before she fell out of the air and held her close to my chest, my heart pounding fast. Brandy jumped up and closed the open window, and I gave her a grateful nod. Aurora immediately started crying, unhappy that I'd stopped her from doing what she wanted, and oblivious to the danger of it all. Fucking hell. How was she flying already?

Lucifer rushed into the room, a sword already forming in his hand, darkness swirling to create the blade. "What's wrong? Is there an attack?"

"We're fine." I glanced down at the baby in my arms who giggled up at me as she moved her wings. "I think."

"Shit." His eyes raked over her and he ran a hand through his hair, blowing out a breath. "Wings? Already?"

"Is that not normal?" Brandy asked, glancing between us.

"No, not at all," I said. "Angels don't get wings 'til they're twenty-one."

"Oh shit," she said.

"Indeed." Lucifer took Aurora from me and held her up, examining her. She quieted down now that her dad held her. "I've never heard of anyone developing wings this young. Sometimes angels do get them early, either at seven or fourteen, but that is extremely rare."

"She's only seven months!" I said, my voice rising with my panic. "How can she have wings already?"

"They're beautiful, though." Lucifer lifted a couple of the black and white feathers and stroked them with care, and Aurora giggled.

A montage of all the ways Aurora could now hurt herself flickered through my mind, and I sank onto the sofa with a groan. Everything needed to remain closed from now on. And locked away. Nothing was safe from her now. "All the childproofing we've done... What use is it now?"

Lucifer lightly tapped Aurora's back between the feathers, and her wings vanished. "We always knew our baby would be special."

"Yes, but I never expected this! Not for many years, anyway."

Brandy handed Isaac another toy. "I don't envy you my friend. Aurora's definitely special, but I can tell she's going to be trouble," she said with a laugh.

Lucifer grinned. "Yes, she is. The best kind of trouble."

I glared at him, worried he wasn't taking this seriously. All our sons had wings, of course, but they'd gotten them at twenty-one. Back then, I'd thought that had been a challenge. Oh past Hannah, how little you knew.

"Let me take her out flying with me," Lucifer said. He'd been asking if he could do it for some time, but I'd been too worried to say yes before. "She'll be perfectly safe in my arms the entire time. She clearly wants to experience the feeling of it, and I can give her a taste of it and show her the proper way to use her wings."

I sighed and rubbed the bridge of my nose. "Fine. Just don't go too far."

26

LUCIFER

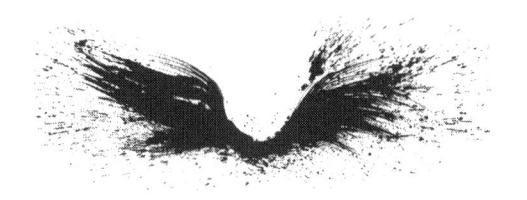

I looked down at Aurora, wrapped snuggly in the fabric Hannah had helped me wind around my body. I was pretty sure Hannah had wrapped us extra tight—more to prevent Aurora from taking off on her own than to ensure I didn't drop her into the ocean. As we flew, I imagined what my enemies would say, seeing the devil with a baby strapped to his chest, but the thought only made me laugh.

Real men wore babies.

Aurora giggled as sea spray coated our faces with a fine mist of salt water, and her little wings moved uselessly against her wrap. Oh, she was trouble, all right. And she wasn't even one yet. How were we going to handle her?

"One more loop around?" I looked down at her, and she shrieked her excitement again as I banked left and swooped a wide arc over the waves. I cupped the top of her head under my palm as water splashed higher than I'd anticipated. I'd never experienced protectiveness quite like this, even with my sons. It was different this time, maybe because she was a girl, or maybe because I knew she would be my last child.

"We need to head back, little one," I said, and she pouted on cue. That face got me every time, and I dipped lower, almost trailing her through the ocean. She shrieked and laughed again, and I chuckled as I smoothed a hand over her wet hair.

"Your Mom's going to kill me for bringing you back drenched in salt water." But I looked at Aurora's face and couldn't find any regret in me. This time together was too precious.

I landed on our carefully manicured lawn, not far from the pool with the tiny Roman-style tiles that Hannah seemed to like. Then, as if thinking about her had summoned her, she burst through the door from the house, running toward me at top speed with a panicked expression on her face.

"Lucifer! There you are!"

Shit. We'd been gone too long, and now I was going to get an earful. I held up my hands in surrender. "We were perfectly safe the entire time, I promise."

"It's not that." Hannah pushed her windswept hair back roughly from her face. "Samael just called. Lilith is missing!"

My heart seemed to stop. "What? Three mates and they can't keep it straight where she is?"

Hannah shook her head. "She was traveling without any of them. All of her guards were found dead. Ripped apart by shifters."

I swore under my breath in languages not spoken on Earth any longer. "Fenrir must have taken her because he knows she has one of the only keys to Hell."

Hannah's eyes widened. "That means they're going after Death. Oh no—Kassiel!"

She sprinted toward the house, and I followed right at her heels. Once inside the kitchen, she grabbed her phone and dialed Kassiel. If Fenrir was trying to release Death, he would need Kassiel—the only person I knew of who could open the tomb, since they'd have to be both born in Hell and carrying the blood of one of the people who had sealed Death away—me, Eve, Michael, and Oberon.

While the phone rang, I unwrapped Aurora. She immediately cried and reached for her mom, and I passed her over to Hannah and took the phone to speak to our son. Luckily, Kassiel answered on the first ring.

"Hey Mom."

"It's me actually."

"Dad?" He always sounded suspicious when I called him.

"Lilith is missing, and Fenrir might be coming for you next. You need to go into hiding. Take Olivia and her other mates with you for protection and leave immediately." There was no point in sugar-coating or small talk. We didn't have time for any of that.

"I understand." Kassiel's tone was serious. "We'll leave right away."

"Get a burner phone in case they're tracking us somehow and check in when you're safe."

"I will."

"Tell him I love him." Hannah touched my arm, her eyebrows draw together.

"I heard," Kassiel said. "I love her too. And you, Dad. Look after my sister, okay?"

My chest swelled with a potent mix of love and fear. "I will. You look after yourself too. Love you, son."

We said goodbye and I turned to Hannah, whose eyes reflected all the same worries I had. It pained me that I couldn't be there physically to protect Kassiel. Maybe I should have had him come here. Or maybe that's what Fenrir expected. Maybe it was better if Kassiel was hiding somewhere that I had no knowledge of. Maybe it was better if he was far from Aurora if shit went down. Maybe not. Fuck. I hated having to make decisions like these.

"Is Kassiel safe?" Hannah cradled Aurora closer, pressing our daughter's head to her shoulder.

"He's as safe as he can be." Then I blew out a sigh. "I need to call Samael."

"I spoke to him just before you returned. He's already sent people to search for Lilith. He's very worried, of course."

I nodded, but knew it wouldn't be enough. Fenrir was too damn crafty, even without Nemesis at his side. "We have to prepare for the worst. If Death is freed..."

Hannah shuddered. "We can't let that happen."

"But if it does, we have no way to stop him once he's released." I closed my eyes as I faced the inevitable. "We have to get the key to Void."

"I thought you might say that." Hannah nodded slowly. "Where is it?"

"In Hell. I hid it in the lowest reaches of our palace before I sealed the realm off. I figured it would be safest there."

Hannah considered this. "The palace is in the equivalent of Egypt. That's a long journey."

"I know. I'll take the private jet and come back as soon as I can."

"No way. I'm coming with you. I don't want to be apart from you for that long. Not after losing you for six months."

"What about Aurora?" I glanced at our baby, at her hands as they grabbed at locks of Hannah's blond hair, at her wings fluttering in excitement. She still wasn't very good at putting them away yet. "That's a long time for us to be away from her."

Hannah shrugged. "She can come with us. Consider it our first family vacation. Besides, despite what Zel thinks, she's safest with us."

I rubbed my chin as I considered it. Hell should be completely empty, but if Fenrir was there waiting for us, we'd probably be able to stop him. After all, we were the Demon King and Queen. Who better to protect our baby in Hell? Whereas if we left her here with Zel, and Fenrir came here looking for us—or for Kassiel—Aurora might be in even more danger. Besides, Hannah and I were a team. After being separated for so long, both in this life and every other, we didn't want to be apart again.

"Very well, we'll go together," I said.

Hannah picked up her phone again. "I'll call Einial and have her make the arrangements."

I took the baby from her as she made the call. The private jet was only a short drive away, but then it would be a long flight to Egypt. Our daughter's first trip.

I hoped it proved to be an uneventful one.

27

HANNAH

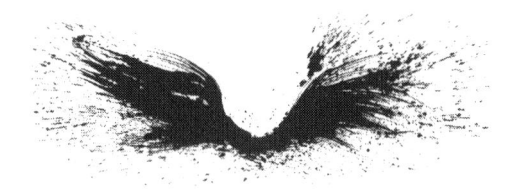

Our palace in Hell was located in the equivalent of the Valley of the Kings. After our private jet landed at Cairo Airport, we checked into our hotel room, and then flew out of the city on our wings under the cover of night. Considering it was her first time away from home, Aurora was doing amazingly well. She slept for some of the flight, and we managed to keep her entertained the rest of the time. Mostly she was just curious about everything she saw. Even now she gazed around from her position on Lucifer's chest, her blue eyes wide as we swooped through the air, hidden from view by the shadows we'd gathered around ourselves.

Once we were out of Cairo, we found an empty patch of desert to cross over into Hell without anyone watching us. We landed gently on the sandy ground, and I glanced around, noting we'd managed to find somewhere actually deserted. "Here?"

"Yes, this should work." Lucifer had a protective arm

across Aurora and he pulled the wrap up to shield her head against the sand that thickened the air. Somewhere along the way she'd fallen asleep, lulled into slumber by the sound of Lucifer's heartbeat and the feel of him gliding through the air.

I stood back as Lucifer produced a gem that seemed to swim with shadows. It emitted a black glow that was almost like the absence of light. A black hole, sucking all light into it.

"The key to Hell." Lucifer lifted it to eye-level, twisting it like he was examining the multi-faceted sides. Then he held it out in front of him and the dark glow spread out and formed an inky black portal before us.

A shiver ran through me as I wondered what I would see on the other side. Last time I'd been in Hell, it had been a battleground, and I'd been fighting for the other side. I also remembered it during our golden years, when I was Persephone and he was Hades and we filled our palace with love and life. I was anxious to see what Hell was like now, after it had been abandoned for so long.

Lucifer entwined his fingers with mine, and together we stepped through the portal into the land of darkness.

People thought Hell was all fire and brimstone, but that was angel propaganda. Hell was an endless night full of twinkling stars and brisk air, with night-blooming flowers that faintly glowed with light and animals that could see in the dark. It was still all of those things as we entered it, but it was also a barren, gray landscape, where instead of the ground being covered with golden sand, flakes of ash drifted into piles and dunes. That was new—there had never been ash, at least not until the angels burned everything down. It pained me knowing I had once been a part of that, before I'd remembered who I really was.

"We're home again." As I spoke, the words settled into my brain with the ring of truth. Just like Heaven and Faerie, this was also my home. Maybe even more so than those places. I'd lived in Hell during so many of my past lives, sometimes for centuries, sometimes for only a few days, but this was my first time visiting as Hannah. Even so, my soul recognized this place as home.

"My domain." Lucifer spread his arms wide as he gazed across the barren landscape. "I've returned."

"You know, since we're bringing Aurora to Hell, we should also take her to Heaven sometime. She needs to connect with her angel heritage as much as her demon one."

He grimaced as a faint shudder worked through him. "You know, I think I've spent far too much time there already recently."

"It'll be different this time. You'll have your family with you."

"We'll discuss this some other time," he conceded, and then let out a low whistle. His horse, Strife, appeared in the distance and rode toward us at top speed, with Shadow just a step behind. We mounted them when they got close, and they took off toward the south, leading us to our first destination.

As we galloped beside the Nile river, my heart sank at the sight of all the destroyed, abandoned buildings, and the complete lack of life anywhere around us. Hell had once been beautiful and prosperous, and it hurt to see it so forlorn. I completely understood why Lucifer had moved all the demons to Earth, since it was the only way to save our people, but it was depressing to see the aftermath of that decision. I stole a glance at Lucifer's face, and judging by his pained expression, he felt the same way.

Soon the great pyramids of Giza appeared in the distance under the soft moonlight, like beacons pulling us toward them. They existed in this realm just as they did on Earth, but with one big difference—in Hell, Death was entombed beneath the Great Sphinx, which was originally built as a monument to him. The entire Giza plateau was once a gateway between the worlds, and the barrier was still weaker here between Earth and Hell, especially with Death's power emanating from the Sphinx. It was no wonder that Giza was thought to be a very haunted place on Earth. The humans might not know why they were both drawn to and revolted by the place, why they went inside only against their better judgment yet couldn't seem to stop themselves—but we did. Death's essence reached across all of the realms, calling to anyone who dared come close to his tomb. It was the one thing no mortal escaped, the last great fear. Even us immortals would succumb to it eventually.

We took some time riding around the pyramids and the Sphinx, checking to make sure Death hadn't been released, but everything was quiet. There was no sign Fenrir or anyone else had been here in decades. I breathed a sigh of relief, until I heard whispered voices on the wind, saying my oldest name.

"Eve...the cursed queen...the lady of many deaths...free me and find peace..."

I shuddered as I tried to block out the horrible words that chilled me to the bone. I was all too familiar with death, and had no interest in experiencing it again. I turned to Lucifer, and his jaw was clenched, his mouth set in a tight line, and I knew he heard something too. What horrible things was Death whispering to him?

"Let's get out of here," I suggested.

Lucifer wrapped Aurora up even tighter, as if he could shield her from the dark presence all around us. "With all haste."

We rode off into the night as fast as our horses would take us, leaving the deathly whispers behind. The other Elder Gods hadn't been able to reach out of their tombs like that, but then again, Death was the most powerful of them all.

We reached our old palace some time later, and the sight of it made my soul weep. The huge columns framing the front were usually alive with climbing plants and flowers that glowed with soft blue light, but now they hung in dead swathes, like tattered drapes from some long-forgotten bygone age. More ash littered the ground, and entire sections of the palace had crumbled to dust.

I flicked my fingers to try to inspire some life in the plants and was rewarded when some veins of green appeared. The plants rustled as they moved, stretching toward me to draw more power, and soon they began to grow again. Tiny little glowing flowers appeared once more, struggling to come back to life. Other than those small movements, the entire place remained desolate and sad, like the soul of the place had died without us here to tend to it.

I sighed and took Lucifer's hand, squeezing it tightly. "I miss this place. I miss what it was."

"I do too." He touched one of the columns as we walked by, his fingers trailing over the smooth black stone. Aurora stirred a little from where she was strapped to his chest and blinked at the glowing flowers with sleepy-eyed interest. "Perhaps we can rebuild once we've got everything else under control."

I turned to him with raised brows. "You would open Hell once more?"

"Someday, yes." He gazed up at a statue of him that was now in pieces. "I've been thinking a lot about this ever since speaking with Belial. Closing Hell and moving all the demons to Earth is one of the reasons the Archdemons revolted against me. Perhaps I shouldn't have been so hasty to close it off completely. At the time, I thought it would be best, just like Michael thought it best to close off Heaven and move the angels to Earth. Both realms were destroyed by our long war, and both races were dying out. We needed to move to Earth to have any chance of survival. But what if that was the wrong decision? I see now that it caused strife for many of our people."

I leaned my head against his shoulder, and stroked Aurora's head where it rested against his chest. "You did what you thought was best for our people at the time, and I know you'll do the best you can going forward, no matter how hard those decisions are to make. Maybe that means starting to rebuild Hell so the demons can return—eventually."

He wrapped an arm around me. "As long as I have you by my side to help me make these decisions going forward."

I shoved him playfully. "Well, obviously."

Aurora began to cry and struggle against Lucifer's chest. After being strapped to him for so long she was probably desperate for some free time, and probably hungry too.

"I'll take her and give her a snack," I said. "You can get the key to Void while we wait outside."

"Probably for the best." Lucifer began unwrapping the baby. "It looks quite dusty inside. I'll be back in a few minutes."

I pulled a blanket out of the diaper bag and set it down, then put Aurora on top of it and began feeding her one of those fruit and veggie pouches that were so convenient. Another thing I wished I'd had in the old days. She devoured it immediately, and I gave her some water, then searched around in the bag for something else to feed her.

Suddenly a growl ripped through the air behind me. I leaped to my feet in front of Aurora, my wings flaring out, with light in one hand and darkness in the other. A three-headed hellhound the size of a horse stood before us, its black fur radiating darkness and its eyes glowing red. Drool dripped from the long, sharp fangs on each of the heads, and sharp claws pawed at the ground as if it might charge us.

"Cerberus, no!" Lucifer cried out, from where he'd appeared in the entrance to the palace.

The hellhound paused, and then launched itself at Lucifer, wagging its tail. Three long tongues came out and covered Lucifer, who held up his hands to defend himself. Aurora giggled and squealed and I made my magic vanish, my shoulders relaxing. Cerberus had been our pet and guardian while in Hell, and it seemed he was still protecting the palace after all these years.

"Down!" Lucifer said, and Cerberus sat and looked up at his master, tail still dancing. Now that the hellhound realized there was no threat to the palace, his demeanor had changed entirely.

"Did you know he was here?" I asked.

Lucifer rubbed Cerberus's many heads. "Yes, he and all of the other hellhounds stayed here when the demons left for Earth. We couldn't exactly bring them along, after all."

"No, I suppose not." I held out a hand and approached him slowly. "Cerberus, it's me. Eve. Persephone. Lenore."

Cerberus tilted his heads, seemingly curious as he examined me. One of his noses sniffed my hand, then he bounced forward, three tongues ready to lick me. I gave him a hug, rubbing the thick fur along his neck.

"It's good to see you too," I said. "Want to meet our newest member of the family?"

Cerberus peered at Aurora next with three big doggy grins, and she giggled and reached for him with both arms. He laid a long lick up her cheek, and she laughed even harder.

"I feel so bad that he's been here all this time." I smoothed a hand along the hellhound's back. "Think he'd like to come home with us?"

Lucifer raised an eyebrow. "A three-headed dog in California?"

"He'd be the perfect guardian and playmate for Aurora." Three pairs of eyes on my child who seemed determined to fly before she could walk sounded perfect at the moment. If we tasked Cerberus with keeping her safe, he' would do everything he could to protect her. "As long as he stays at the estate, it should be fine."

"I can't argue with that." Lucifer patted Cerberus on the back. "Do you want to come back with us, old boy? We could use your help defending a new palace."

Cerberus let out a bark and wagged his tail harder, and I guessed that meant yes.

"It's settled then," Lucifer said.

I began packing up all of Aurora's things, eager to leave this forlorn place. "Did you get the key to Void?"

"Yes, I did." Lucifer held up a small velvet drawstring bag, then tucked it into a pocket. "Let's go home."

I glanced back at the palace that had once been our home. Perhaps one day it would be again. But for the moment, our place was on Earth.

28

HANNAH

Cerberus nudged Aurora across the floor, butt-scooting her along with one of his noses, and her peals of laughter rang out around the nursery. Even Zel smiled at the close bond that had developed between them.

Lucifer wrapped an arm around my waist, drawing me closer. He nuzzled a kiss to my neck. "Think anyone would notice if we took an hour for ourselves?"

I lifted an eyebrow as I grinned. "A whole hour? What a luxury that would be."

He laughed and kissed my neck again, but then his phone rang, and he cursed under his breath. "It's Samael."

I nodded, my smile dropping immediately. It had been a week since we'd gotten back from Hell, and there had been no news about Lilith's whereabouts. "You'd better get it then."

Lucifer huffed out a sigh as he answered. "Hello,

Samael. Everything all right?" He paused and his eyes landed on me. "Yes, she's here."

I turned to Zel, worry already nagging at my gut. "Could you watch Aurora while we take this?"

"Of course," Zel said.

Lucifer and I headed out of the nursery and into our bedroom, shutting the door behind us. I sat on the edge of the bed as Lucifer tapped his phone and said, "Okay, we're ready."

"We have an emergency here in Vegas," Samael's deep voice said from the phone's speaker. "Pestilence has been freed and we're under attack."

"What?" I asked, jumping to my feet again.

"How?" Lucifer asked.

"Our cameras show it was Theo who released him," Samael said.

Theo? I gripped Lucifer's forearm. No, that made no sense. Theo had been my guard for months. I trusted him with my life. He'd helped me become Famine, and he'd been there when we sealed Pestilence inside. Why would he free Pestilence now?

"Are you sure it was him?" I asked, my voice trembling a little.

"We're sure." Samael spoke on a sigh, the words almost an apology. "We need your help. Pestilence is attacking The Celestial as we speak. Our people managed to evacuate it as best we could, but I fear he's going to spread his plague to everyone in Las Vegas within a few hours."

"We'll be there in an hour," Lucifer said, before hanging

up. It wasn't even a question of whether we would go or not. We were the only ones who could stop Pestilence—especially if the gargoyles had turned on us. And with the tomb no longer an option, our only hope was to use the Void key to send Pestilence to that realm.

I glanced around the room, wondering if I should pack anything or change my clothes, and instead opted for just throwing on my sneakers and a bra. Would anyone care if the Queen of Hell showed up to fight Pestilence in yoga pants? Probably not. Assuming anyone was even alive by the time we got there.

I rushed back into the nursery, where Aurora was riding on Cerberus's back while Zel fed the hellhound a biscuit. My chest tightened as the reality of the situation sunk in, and I accepted that I would have to leave Aurora behind. It was too dangerous for her to go with us this time. She would be safer here. I knew that, but it was still hard to leave her.

"We have to go to Vegas," I said, as I grabbed Aurora and pulled her against my chest. "Pestilence is free."

"Oh fuck." Zel rose to her feet. "Do you need me to go?"

"No, I need you to stay here and watch Aurora." I felt a slight pang of guilt that one of the greatest warriors of all time was relegated to babysitter duty, but there was no one else I would trust more with my daughter.

Zel nodded. "That I can do. Cerberus and I will keep her safe."

"Thank you." I hugged Aurora to my chest, kissing her face a hundred times. "Mommy will be back soon, I promise. I love you so much."

Lucifer came into the nursery and took Aurora from me, then said his own goodbyes while I wrung my hands nervously. We'd never left her behind before. Not even for date night. Not while Fenrir was still out there. Now we were going into certain danger, and there was no other option but to leave her here.

I took Aurora again and gave her more kisses and hugs, then reluctantly handed her to Zel. I opened my mouth to tell Zel about bedtime and what to feed her and everything else I could think of, but Zel held up a hand to stop me.

"I got this. Go save the world."

I hugged her close, then walked out of the room with Lucifer. We got in our Lamborghini, and Lucifer drove out of the estate so fast the world became almost a blur around us. The private jet waited at a nearby airstrip, and Lucifer was already on the phone telling them to get it ready to go.

When he hung up, we settled into uneasy silence. Finally I said, "I can't believe Theo did this."

"Another traitor," Lucifer said with disgust. "Maybe he thinks he's continuing his mother's plans after her death."

"That would mean he's been waiting all this time for the right moment to act." I swallowed hard, feeling the sting of his betrayal deep inside.

Lucifer shook his head. "I didn't know him as well as you did, so I can't say for sure. But we always knew there could be gargoyles who believed so earnestly in Belphegor's mission that her death wouldn't stop their actions. Theo might be one of them."

"And Romana?"

"I think she is loyal." Lucifer sighed, his hands gripping the steering wheel so tight his knuckles were white. "I guess we'll find out soon enough."

I nodded and stared out the window as we zoomed down the highway. "I hate that we have to leave Aurora."

"She'll be all right," Lucifer said, his voice gentle. "Zel will be there, along with Cerberus. Neither of them will let anything happen to her."

"I know. And our estate's well-guarded and has plenty of security measures in place... I still hate it."

"Me too." He rested a hand on my thigh. "We'll take care of this problem and be back in no time."

I prayed he was right. I'd gotten so used to our perfect, happy, almost-normal life, but deep down I'd known it could never last. A threat would always emerge that we would have to face, and every time we would be forced to leave Aurora behind, knowing we might not come back. It had been the same during all of my lives. No wonder all of our sons had issues. We'd done the best we could with them, but we'd always had other duties too, duties that were so important we couldn't pass them off to other people. It was hard being a parent when you had to save the world all the time. I hadn't really understood that until now, and I feared we would repeat the same mistakes with Aurora. But what else could we do?

Stopping Pestilence would help, for a start. Adam had been a threat during all of my kids' lives, and if he were finally out of the picture, we could relax a little. It was time to take the fucker down.

29

LUCIFER

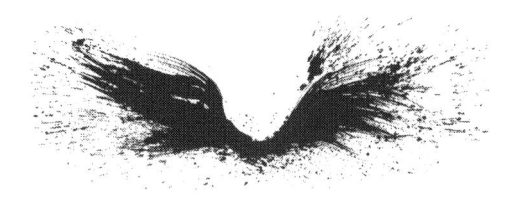

I tightened my thighs to spur Strife on as we left the airport and headed into downtown Las Vegas. We'd known something was wrong before the jet even touched down, as the sun glinted off the buildings bold enough to stretch their glassy tips farthest into the sky. This city was an oasis of life in the middle of the Nevada desert, but even from a distance, we could tell that Vegas was sick. Plumes of black smoke rose from various spots along The Strip, and I feared what we would find when we returned to The Celestial.

As we drew closer to my resort, the extent of the damage became clearer. Windows had been blown out, bodies were strewn across the pavement and covered in boils, and even the plants had withered and died from the sickness in the air. Our horses brought us to Hannah's garden that had once thrived with life, but now everything here was dead, the flowers black, the leaves spotted and brown. Up ahead, the waterfall recycled murky yellow water, and behind it was a huge hole where Pestilence's tomb had been hidden away. The tomb itself was gone. Or destroyed. I wasn't sure. But where was Pestilence?

Hannah surveyed the damage in the garden she'd created, her fingers flickering idly over various plants, coaxing life back into them, although the movement didn't seem to be deliberate on her part. She looked absolutely horrified by it all, her face paler than normal, her eyes wet with unshed tears, especially when her gaze landed on the tourists that had died. Entire families, destroyed by Pestilence's plague. Intense rage filled me at the sight. These people had come to my hotel for a family vacation or a fun weekend getaway and now they were dead. It was my responsibility to keep them safe and happy while at my resort, and I'd failed. Now all I could do was avenge their deaths...which I would do with relish.

Sirens sounded from the street, and the sound of human misery and suffering thickened the air. I kept the War side of me locked away most of the time, but now I let it surface. The fury made me stronger, as long as I could control it.

"I'm going to rip Adam's fucking head off," I growled.

Hannah shot me a look full of menace. "Not if I do it first."

"We need to find Samael. Let's check the war room."

Hannah nodded, and our wings unfurled at the same time, mine black and shadowy, hers silver and bright. We launched into the air and flew up to the penthouse, which had sat empty for months, but had been destroyed anyway.

Pestilence had even peed all over my leather couch. That fucking prick. Hannah just let out a long sigh as she surveyed the damage.

We marched down the stairs rather than take the elevator, uncertain of the electrics and stability of the infrastructure. I'd never seen my command room so busy. Demons scurried between desks and spoke into headsets while typing furiously on their computers. Lights flashed on monitors and maps, showing the activity of my demons across the city and wider areas. Occasionally, alarms went off, attracting more frenetic activity at various desks.

Samael watched over everything, his arms folded tightly across his chest, his face expressionless but his jaw tight. He turned toward us as we approached, and something that looked like relief flickered across his features before he clamped down on it and returned to being expressionless. He nodded a greeting, and I motioned toward the meeting room. We'd be able to watch from within the glass walls without being overheard.

"What's happening?" Hannah spoke first—as soon as the door closed.

"Where is Pestilence?" I asked.

"You're too late," Samael said. "He's gone."

"Gone?" Hannah asked. "Where did he go?"

"No one knows. He rode off on his horse into the desert."

"And Theo?" I asked. Another fucker who needed to die.

"Also gone. He left as soon as Pestilence was freed, and took many of the gargoyles with him."

Dammit. We were too late. Pestilence had gone, leaving

destruction and sickness in his wake. My vengeance would have to wait another day.

"Where's Einial?" Hannah asked. Normally she was at Samael's side, helping him run things.

Samael's face fell. "Dead. Killed by Theo when she tried to stop him from opening Pestilence's tomb."

Hannah covered her mouth with her hand, her eyes wide. "Oh no. I'm so sorry."

"Pestilence will pay for what he's done," I growled. "What about the humans?"

"We've put word out about a terrorist attack," Samael said. "Chemical weapons. It's something the humans will believe and rally behind."

"Good thinking." It wasn't like any of them would believe that demon factions were currently releasing the Four Horsemen of the Apocalypse, or that Pestilence had destroyed much of the Las Vegas Strip. "What can we do?"

"We've got everything in hand here, but you can speak to the press perhaps. Or try to find Pestilence, though I'm not sure how you'll locate him."

I agreed, but Pestilence's disappearance grated against me. "It's surprising he left so quickly. He must have known that Hannah and I would come for him. Wouldn't he want to face us? To try to take Hannah, if nothing else?"

"Maybe that's why he left," Samael said. "He knew he couldn't face both of you together."

Hannah tapped her lips. "Maybe... Or maybe he's going to meet Fenrir somewhere for the real attack."

Her words sparked a horrible idea inside my head. "What if this was all a diversion?"

Hannah's eyes widened. "What do you mean?"

"It's possible." Samael stroked his chin. "There's certainly enough damage control here to keep us all busy for a while."

"And it got us both away from home." Hannah gripped my arm tightly, her voice rising with her panic. "We need to get back to Aurora."

I nodded, heart pounding, gut twisting with fear. "Samael, you've got this covered. We need to return home."

"Go," Samael said. "I'll keep you updated on any new developments."

I nodded and clasped Samael's shoulder briefly before Hannah and I left the room at a near run. I tried to keep my panic in check, but instinct told me something wasn't right, and that things were about to get a lot worse.

Then again, things getting worse was a given until we found Pestilence.

Hannah whipped across the grass on Shadow, always a couple of hoofbeats ahead of me like she was being chased by hellhounds rather than simply returning home. I felt that same urgency and urged Strife on too.

"Are you all right?" I shouted my words into the wind racing past, hoping Hannah heard me.

"No." It was one word tossed over her shoulder. "I have a really bad feeling."

"Me too."

She remained silent the rest of the ride, but there was a tension in her posture as she sat on Shadow's back, and her face could have called forth thunder.

We arrived at our estate, but Hannah didn't even wait for Shadow to slow before she leapt off her back and took off toward our house. That's when I realized how quiet and empty it was on our estate. Something was wrong. Worse than Vegas.

Death lingered here.

"Hannah—wait!"

But she sped up, my call spurring her on rather than holding her back. She pushed the front door open and screamed.

I was with her within moments. Two of our guards lay dead on the hardwood floor, their bodies lying there peacefully, as if they'd gone to sleep and never woken up. There was no sign of a struggle. An unnatural quiet blanketed the house, and the air was too still.

"Aurora! Zel! Cerberus!" Hannah ran from room to room, her voice going shrill as she screamed the names over and over. I searched too, my heart in my throat, my fear so strong I couldn't say anything at all. We checked everywhere. The bedrooms. The office. The kitchen. The pool.

The nursery.

The house was empty aside from dozens of dead guards. There was not one single living person on the estate, as far as I could tell, though nothing else had been touched.

Hannah was in a complete panic, her eyes wild. "Where is Aurora?"

I shook my head and drew her into my arms, partly to keep myself from falling apart. "I don't know."

"Or Zel? Or Cerberus?"

I had no answer to that either. As I'd searched the house, I'd been terrified that I might find one—or all—of them dead, just like the guards. It was a small relief—very small—that they weren't here. They could still be alive. Taken by whoever had done this.

Oh, who was I kidding? I knew who'd done this. Of course I did. The presence was unmistakable, even after thousands of years apart. I smelled it lingering in the air, heard the ghostly whispers on the breeze, and felt the eerie chill trailing down my spine.

Death.

My father.

Somehow he was free—and he'd taken my daughter.

30

HANNAH

Everything inside me screamed and sobbed. It was a miracle I wasn't doing both of those on the outside too, but I was using every ounce of control I had to keep it together. Falling apart wouldn't save Aurora, and I had to act quickly. I had to do everything I could to find her, even if all I wanted to do was break into a million pieces.

Lucifer threw his arms out to the side and let out a guttural roar that made the windows of the house shake. His eyes were red, and fury radiated off of him in menacing waves. The part of him that was War was emerging. I considered stopping it and trying to calm him down, but then said fuck it. If there was ever a time to be Famine and War, it was now.

"We'll get her back," I told him, as my own desperation brought out my endless hunger and thirst. This time, it was an all-consuming yearning to save her. A mirror across from me showed that my eyes were glowing green too, and I embraced the power. To save my daughter I would become a force to be reckoned with. I would tear apart the entire world if I had to, if that's what it took to find her.

Yes. I could do this. I'd rescued Lucifer from War, for fuck's sake. I could find my daughter, a three-headed dog, and my demon bodyguard. It wasn't like they'd be easy to hide, and it must have been Fenrir who'd taken them. This didn't look like a shifter attack, but who else could it have been?

A noise stirred behind us, like the sound of people moving and the rustle of fabric. Lucifer and I shared a "what now?" look, before we turned to face whatever this was from our spot in the middle of the living room. But what I saw made my stomach drop.

The dead guards around us rose to their feet, their completely black eyes staring at us. As they stepped forward, their movements were jerky, unnatural, and they raised their weapons in threat. From the corner of my eye I saw more coming down the staircase, and others in the garden and by the pool heading toward us. They said nothing, but their intent was clear, and Lucifer and I summoned our magic to defend ourselves.

The undead guards threw themselves at us with abandon, slashing their weapons and shooting their guns, even though there was no chance they could win against us. A cocktail of terror and grief mixed inside me as we fought them off with blasts of light and darkness. But every time we knocked them down, they got back up again.

All right then. I'd seen enough zombie movies in my

time as a human, and I knew there was one surefire way to stop the undead. I created twin swords of twisting light and darkness for myself and for Lucifer, which easily sliced off the heads of our former guards. I felt sick to my stomach as I took them down, these men and women who had once worked to protect us, but were now being used against us. I knew they were already dead, but I hated it anyway. I remembered all of their names. Every single one of them. And they'd died because of us.

One of the guards suddenly stopped before us and croaked out with a rasping voice, "Death awaits you in Hell."

"What did you just say?" I asked, as a chill ran through me.

"If you want your daughter back, come find him," the undead continued.

Lucifer sprang forward and sliced his sword through the guard's neck. The head tumbled to the floor and rolled across the hardwood, scattering small droplets of blood everywhere.

That was the last of them. I vanished our swords, my hands shaking as the horrible truth of the guard's words sank into me. I turned to Lucifer and met his angry gaze, my eyes wide. "Death took Aurora?"

"Yes, it must be him." Lucifer spoke through gritted teeth. "He's been freed somehow."

Another horrible realization hit me, and my panic spiked again. "Kassiel!"

Lucifer reached into his inside jacket pocket and withdrew his phone. "Call him."

I took the phone with shaking hands. If Death had been released, Kassiel had to have been there. They needed his blood—and he wouldn't have gone willingly. So how much blood had they spilled? Was he still alive?

The screen blurred and I could barely read the list of contacts. Lucifer took the phone back and tapped it a couple of times before handing it to me. As it rang, I drew a shaky breath, and when Kassiel answered, I blew it all back out in a hurry.

"Kassiel?"

"Mom?"

The sound of his voice filled me with relief. "Are you okay? Where are you?"

"I'm fine. We're still in hiding. Why, Mom? What's happened?"

"He's okay," I said to Lucifer, and my husband closed his eyes, his jaw visibly relaxing. I hit a button so Lucifer could hear too as I asked Kassiel, "Are you safe where you are? Are the others with you?"

"Yes, they're all here. What's going on?"

"They've released Death," Lucifer said. "And he took your sister."

"What?" Kassiel yelled from the other side of the phone. "Where?"

"To Hell." Lucifer tensed again, his hands curling into fists, his knuckles going white. "Death wants us to find him there."

"Then I'm coming with you," Kassiel said. "We all are."

I tensed at the thought of putting another of my children

in danger, but we would need his help. We would need everyone's help to face what we were up against. "We'll let you know when we have a plan. Stay safe."

We told Kassiel we loved him and then hung up. As soon as I did, Lucifer spun away from me, a cry of rage tearing from him as he conjured a shadow blade from nowhere and smashed it against the fireplace. Then the dining table. And the sofa.

He raised the weapon again and I yelled, "Stop! Destroying our house won't get her back!"

Lucifer looked at me, his gaze a burning mix of fury and grief. In his eyes, I saw the same desperate pain resonating within me, and knew he would burn the entire world down if that's what it would take to get Aurora back. I'd let him do it too. I'd throw on the gasoline and strike the matches. With Lucifer at my side, I'd become the villain, the terrifying goddess of hunger and misery, the bringer of the apocalypse. All to save our child.

"We'll find her." I held out my hands to Lucifer, and his blade disappeared before he walked over to me. He slid his fingers into mine, and we stared back at each other with resolve. A new strength straightened my spine as power rippled along my skin, moving back and forth between me and Lucifer. Ancient power. Godly power. "We're Lucifer and Hannah. Demon King and Queen. War and Famine. No one can stop us, not when we're together."

Lucifer nodded slowly, his rage shifting to determination, his hands squeezing mine. "We've fought together for all of time, and we won't let anyone take what's ours. I'll make the calls and rally the troops. If Death wants us to meet him in Hell, we're bringing an army with us."

Our horses appeared just outside the open sliding glass doors, their eyes glowing like ours were as they angrily stomped their hooves and shook their heads. They were ready for battle too.

We were Horsemen, and it was time for the apocalypse to begin. *Our* apocalypse.

31

HANNAH

We were back in Egypt, but this time Aurora wasn't giggling happily from her usual position on Lucifer's chest, and my heart ached at the loss of her. The Great Sphinx loomed over us under a moonless night that cloaked us in darkness, and just as well, because Lucifer and I had gathered all of our allies here at the Giza Pyramids.

We had an army.

With Lucifer at my side, we made the rounds to make sure everyone was ready and knew what to do before we opened the portal to Hell. Once on the other side, everything would happen fast, and it would all be chaos. As we walked across ancient sand-beaten stones, I shivered, but not from the cold. Death truly did linger around this crumbling monument, even here on Earth.

Samael hovered nearby, staring at his phone like he was still considering the logistics and organization of the mission —always one step ahead and completely reliable under every circumstance. It made me sad seeing him without his assistant Einial, which only increased my resolve to avenge her death. She'd been good to me while Lucifer was in Heaven, and it was a damn shame she'd been another of Pestilence's casualties.

"Everything is ready," Samael said, when he finally noticed us approaching. "We only await your command."

There was a touch of sadness in his eyes I hadn't seen before. I stepped forward and gave him a hug, realizing he was also worried for a loved one. "I'm sure Lilith is with them."

"I hope you're right." Samael blew out a breath. "She went with them willingly, so perhaps they haven't harmed her. Baal got the full story from their daughter, Lena. Fenrir kidnapped them both, and Lilith agreed to use the key to open the portal to Hell only after Lena was released and her safety assured."

"I can't fault her for doing that to save her daughter," I said with a sigh. Not when I stood here with an entire army to rescue Aurora. Mothers moved mountains. We always would.

Baal and Gabriel stood a short distance away among a few other vampires and angels, all donning their weapons and armor. Baal wore black and red armor with spikes, befitting a vampire lord, while Gabriel wore gleaming golden armor perfect for an Archangel. Together, they looked particularly formidable as they prepared to go into battle to rescue the woman they loved. As Gabriel raised his spear, I'd never seen the Archangel look so foreboding, and I had a sudden flash of what he'd be like if he'd become Fallen instead of Lucifer.

After a few more words with Samael, we moved to speak with Romana, who stood in gargoyle form, her bat-like wings folded behind her. She barked commands to the gargoyle soldiers in front of her, and then turned toward us with blazing eyes. She wore Theo's betrayal like a shroud, like it had personally stained her, and now she had the ferocity of a woman with a lot to prove.

She bowed toward us. "My king and queen, I wish to apologize for my brother's actions."

"There is nothing to apologize for," Lucifer said.

"We know you weren't involved in his betrayal," I added.

Romana shook her head, her mouth twisted in an angry scowl. "No, but I should have seen it coming. Theo was always Belphegor's most loyal child, and I think he believed he should have become Archdemon instead of me, even though I am older than him by many centuries, and..."

"And what?" I asked, sensing there was more to this story.

Romana glanced about, and when she spoke again, she'd lowered her voice. "Theo is not entirely demon. He is half angel. Archangel, to be precise."

Lucifer arched an eyebrow. "Who is his father?"

"Michael," Romana said, her voice barely above a whisper.

My mouth fell open. That would make him Callan's half-brother. Lucifer tensed beside me too at the name.

Romana continued speaking in a low voice, as if telling us a secret. "He and Belphegor had a short fling about two hundred years ago, long before there was peace between the angels and demons. Theo was raised in Hell by our mother, who kept his parentage a secret. According to her, Michael refused to acknowledge Theo as his son. It's one of the reasons Mother hated angels so much, and why Theo hates them still."

"Michael's son, born in Hell..." Lucifer said, then closed his eyes and nodded. "That must be how they opened Death's tomb."

Of course. They hadn't needed Kassiel at all because they had Theo all along, carrying the blood of one of the people who had sealed away Death originally. Damn. If only we'd known the truth about him sooner.

It was too late to worry about what we might have done differently. I touched Romana's arm lightly. "Thank you for coming today, Romana. I know it's hard to be divided in your loyalties."

She stood up straight, her leathery wings twitching. "There is no division. My brother will be brought to justice for what he's done. As will the rest of them."

Lucifer began to speak, but he was interrupted by a colorful portal opening up in the sand. My mother stepped through it wearing elaborate, shining armor with flowers engraved on the breastplate and along the arms and legs. Her helmet was designed to look like an armored crown, and she carried a staff in her hand. Damien left the portal right behind her in his own similar armor, and with him were about a dozen other soldiers from the Spring Court. My people, once.

I rushed over to them and gave my son a big hug, then turned to my mother. She embraced me too, to my surprise.

"Daughter," she said, as she stroked my back. "I understand your pain all too well."

"We came as soon as we heard," Damien said. "We're here to help get Aurora back."

Demeter pulled back from me and regained her composure immediately. "The Spring Court will not sit idly by while one of our own is attacked. And unlike Oberon, we will not ignore a threat that will spread to all of the realms if not stopped now."

"I'm so glad you're here," I said, glancing between the two of them. "Both of you."

"Yes, thank you." Lucifer moved up behind me and nodded at my mother. "We gladly welcome the help of the Spring Court in this battle."

Demeter offered him a smile that was more winter than spring... But it was a start.

Damien waved at Kassiel and Belial, who were standing with Olivia, Marcus, Callan, and Bastien. We headed toward them, leaving Demeter behind with her soldiers, and Olivia threw her arms around me.

"I'm so sorry about Aurora," she said, as she squeezed me close.

Callan pulled me in for a big bear hug next. "I'll do whatever I can to get my niece back. We're family, after all."

"Yes, we are," I said, wondering when I should tell him

about Theo. Maybe when this was all over, if any of us were still alive. Instead, I turned to give my thanks to Marcus and Bastien.

Kassiel wrapped an arm around me, and we moved over to speak with Damien and Belial. I gazed at my three sons, noting how different they were. Damien in his fae court armor, his blue-black hair flowing in the wind. Kassiel in a suit much like his father's, and sharing the same green eyes. Belial in ripped-up jeans, motorcycle boots, with Morningstar strapped to his back. I loved them all so much, and though I worried about each of them getting hurt in the upcoming battle, I accepted that they were grown men too. If they wanted to fight for their family, who was I to stop them?

"Don't do anything stupid and get yourselves killed, or I'll kick your asses," Belial said to his brothers.

"That doesn't even make sense," Kassiel replied with a shake of his head.

Damien gave his brothers a mischievous smirk. "He's just worried we're going to steal all the glory in the battle."

Belial crossed his arms. "Hardly."

"Just be careful out there," I couldn't help but add. I was still their mother, after all. "I love you all so much."

Kassiel rested a hand on my shoulder, his demeanor going serious. "Don't worry. We'll get Aurora back."

"Yes, we will," Lucifer said, gazing at his sons with unabashed pride. "On that note, I have tasks for the three of you I can't trust with anyone else. Kassiel and Damien, I need you to find Azazel, Lilith and Cerberus. Free them and get them to safety."

"It will be done," Damien said.

Lucifer looked at Belial for a few seconds before he spoke, his words heavy. "Belial, I need you to rescue your sister. Your mother and I will be busy fighting Death and Pestilence. We need you to keep Aurora safe."

"I swear it on my life." Belial pressed a fist to his heart. "On my very soul."

They stared at each other and I sensed that the enormity of Lucifer's trust in Belial had lifted a great weight between them.

Then it was time to begin. We hugged our sons again, and moved to stand in the center of the Giza plateau between the pyramids. Lucifer wore black and silver armor along with a spiked crown covered in rubies, and his entire body glowed with a slight red tint. Beside him, I wore the gold and silver armor I'd once donned as an angel, except I now wore a matching crown to Lucifer's, although mine had emeralds for the gemstones.

All of the people assembled before us quieted down, waiting for the Demon King and Queen to speak. I gazed out across the soldiers we'd gathered, an impressive mix of angel, demon, and fae, all willing to fight and die to rescue the people we loved and save the world from the impending apocalypse that Pestilence and Death would bring.

I waited for Lucifer to begin, but he gestured for me to take the lead. I cleared my throat and raised my voice, infusing it with power so it would boom out into the night.

"Death has been released. He's free and he's waiting for us in Hell, and he's taken my daughter and my friends. We must stop both him and Pestilence to prevent the apocalypse they will bring to all the realms. They have powerful allies, but we have an army too. One built of love and respect, not of fear and anger. Because of that, we will succeed. I have no doubt."

A roar rippled through the crowd, growing louder as the soldiers gathered before us fed from each other's enthusiasm. Famine reached for their power until I almost glowed from it, though I made sure to send it back to them. They would need all their strength for this upcoming battle.

"We have a plan." At the sound of Lucifer's voice, everyone fell immediately silent. "We must stop this threat today, before Pestilence and Death spread their evil to the other worlds. I will open a portal to Void, and Hannah and I will force Pestilence and Death through it, while the rest of you keep their forces busy. Once they're through, we must close the portal to Void immediately, to make sure no other Elder Gods enter our world." He looked at me with love and devotion. "Failure is not an option, but we won't fail. They may have two Horsemen, but so do we. Let's show them what our apocalypse looks like."

With that, Lucifer held out the key to Hell and a huge black, shadowy portal opened up. Big enough for many soldiers to enter at once. I spread my silver wings, and Lucifer spread his shadowy ones beside me, and together we flew into Hell to save our daughter—and defeat two Gods.

32

LUCIFER

My army poured through the portal into Hell, with Hannah and myself in the lead. The air on this side was colder, the sky was darker, and the scent of death was everywhere.

Death lounged on a throne under the head of the Great Sphinx. My fucking throne, which he must have had brought over from the palace just to spite me. He wore Fenrir's body, and I wondered what the Archdemon had sacrificed in order to gain Death's power. His eyes shone an eerie purple, and his body had already begun changing, becoming almost...skeletal.

What a fool. There was too much power for Fenrir to even stand a chance against Death. He couldn't contain it, never mind control it. Not that he wanted to. All Fenrir wanted was to destroy me and take my place as king, and it seemed his interests aligned with my father's.

I held up a hand to halt my forces behind me as I took in

what we were facing. Pestilence—Adam—stood to the right of my father, and on the other side of him was Theo. War's fury bubbled up inside me as I thought of all the things I wanted to do to them, but then my gaze landed on the cages just behind them. They were all made of jagged bone that looked like it had sprung up out of the ground and then been bent and twisted to Death's will. Inside each cage was someone I cared about deeply. Lilith. Azazel. Cerberus.

Aurora.

She made her way around her cage, her black and white wings fluttering to keep her airborne as she bumped her head against the bones with each jerky ascent. My rage became a volcano inside me about to explode at the sight, and Hannah's hand tightened around mine, letting me know she'd seen it too.

I forced myself to look away, to study the horde my father had amassed all around us under the shadow of the pyramids. Shifters, imp, gargoyles, and others who had decided to defy their Archdemon to fight me. Their forces surrounded ours, but we could take them. Fuck, I could probably take them single-handedly with my rage at seeing Aurora in a cage. I was barely in control of myself, and Hannah gripped me tighter like she knew that. Fury burned through me, and I took a deep breath as Hannah and I landed in front of my father.

Death's laugh boomed from Fenrir's mouth, and it sounded wet, like something inside him was broken. "So good of you to join me, Lucifer."

"Father." I looked straight at him as I greeted him, giving

him the honor of our relationship without making myself submissive to him. I wouldn't bow and scrape to Death, but I could remind him we were family once.

"And Eve, in a new body." Death tilted his head as he studied her.

"Thanatos," she said in a low, menacing voice. I was impressed she remembered his name from all those years ago.

His haunting eyes landed on me again. "I see you finally broke the curse. Certainly took you long enough."

My hands clenched into fists at my side at the reminder of what he'd done to us all those centuries ago. How he'd managed to haunt us even while locked in a tomb for thousands of years.

"Not all of us are so eager to bring death upon those we love," I said through gritted teeth.

"You always were weak." Death raised himself from my throne like he still hadn't gotten used to controlling a body and all of the articulated joints yet. He rolled rather than walked toward us, his limbs strangely fluid. "No matter. I've taken over as the rightful King of Hell, a role that's been vacant since you saw fit to abandon this realm."

"I am still the King of Hell."

He laughed again. "Don't waste your breath. Your people need someone strong to lead them, someone who will rebuild Hell and make it a true land of the dead. Once that is done, I'll spread my kingdom to Earth, then to Heaven and Faerie." He indicated the angels and the fae in my army. "How nice of you to bring representatives."

"We're not going to let you do that," Hannah said.

"Why would you stop me?" His eyes narrowed as he studied us closer. "Even if you could, which we all know is impossible, you are War and Famine. Your purpose is to serve me, the leader of the Horsemen, as we take over all the worlds and remake them in our image." He indicated everyone around us, and gestured wider still, like he could encompass all of the realms. "Come, let us rule together. The Four Horsemen of the Apocalypse, as prophesied, as it should be." He stretched his mouth into a grin. A grimace. A leer. "We can put the past behind us."

"Hannah and I will never work with you," I replied. It wasn't like I was being presumptuous, speaking for my mate. Not when our baby was trapped in a fucking cage made of bones.

"Give me my daughter back." Hannah spoke in a voice like steel. It was a cold, hard demand, but Death laughed again.

"I can't do that." He stole a quick look over his shoulder and flicked Aurora a small wave, just a little movement of his fingers. "I have big plans for my granddaughter."

"What plans?" I asked.

"I'm going to raise her as my own. My little prodigy. A perfect blend of light and dark with the added essence of an Elder God. She will learn from me and rule by my side. She'll be the child you weren't, the child you could never be. And one day, when she's older, she'll be the perfect host."

"You fucking bastard." As if I didn't already have enough reason to stuff him into the Void. No way was he raising my daughter to be his next body. "You won't harm a hair on her body, and you won't rule anything, because we're stopping you today."

"You can't stop Death. I'm inevitable."

"We'll see about that." I gave my army the signal they'd been waiting for, and they let out a triumphant roar and began to march forward. I turned to Belial, who'd landed just behind me, and handed him the key to Hell. "If anything happens, get our family out of here."

He nodded and flew off toward the cages, with his brothers beside him. It was the only thing I could do to make sure they were safe should Hannah and I fail. Of course, if we failed, nowhere would be safe. Not from Death.

Hannah and I shared a look, one of love and devotion and fierce determination, and I pulled her close and kissed her hard, in case it was the last time. She clung to me tightly like she would never let me go, and then we stepped back.

She sighed as she glanced toward the throne. "Time to save the world again."

"I'll take my father. You deal with Pestilence."

"Gladly," she said. "I love you."

"I love you too. Always."

I released my wings and let my fury free, feeling it race through my body, dragging heat and electricity with it. I crackled with rage, and the part of me that was War gave me strength. It reminded me that even before I was War I was made for battle, forged from death and light to be the fiercest of Heaven's warriors, then remade into the Prince of Darkness, the Father of Lies, the King of Demons.

If anyone could defeat Death, it was me.

33

HANNAH

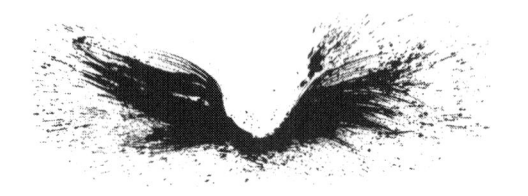

As Lucifer and I flew toward Death, the monster lifted his arms and a wave of power rolled out of him. It didn't do anything to the two of us, nor to our soldiers, but instead settled over the land with a murky purple light. Mere seconds later, skeletal hands burst out of the ground as corpses came back to life. Dust gathered and reformed into undead soldiers, both angels and demons who had perished over thousands of years during the Great War. Others were more recent corpses, their skin hanging off or in various stages of decay, their wings ragged, their light long extinguished. They charged toward our army, along with the others Death and Pestilence had gathered to fight for them.

Zel rattled the bones of her cage uselessly, her face a mask of rage as Pestilence spread sickness over the shifters rushing forward. Boils broke out over their skin and they became graying, dying shadows of themselves. They raced in among our army, becoming walking contagions. Theo leaped up on his leather wings and flew into battle with them, his stone skin protecting him from Pestilence's plague.

The roaring cries of war filled the air as angels, demons, fae, and undead collided, but I only had eyes for one man. Adam. He'd killed me repeatedly, time after time ripping me away from Lucifer and my children. He'd killed my last daughter before she'd even had a chance to live. Now he threatened my other daughter's life, and I wasn't letting him get away with it this time.

He was mine.

As battle raged behind me, I ignored the clash of swords and claws and the blasts of magic. I had only one duty—to stop Pestilence, while Lucifer stopped Death. It came down to the two of us. No one else could do this, and we couldn't fail. We wouldn't. I was too fucking mad. Not just because they'd taken my daughter, but because of everything Adam and Death had done to me for thousands of years, going back to my very first life as Eve. They'd tormented me enough, and I was done. So fucking done.

Adam's face was a nightmare of yellow skin and puss-filled boils, his grin a gash in his face. I landed in front of him and formed my sword of darkness entwined with light.

"So nice of you to return to me, Eve," he said, as he drew his golden bow and arrows. "I'd like you to know I've given up on convincing you to rule by my side."

I snorted. "That's a relief."

"Is it? Because now the only other option is for you to die." He shot a plague-tipped arrow at me, but I used a blast of wind to shoot it wide. He hadn't really intended on hitting me with it though. He was just taunting me. "I'll take the most pleasure from your death this time, I think. Maybe I'll even fuck your corpse when it's done. One last time, just you and me, like the old days."

I leveled my sword at him, trying not to gag at his words. "You disgust me—and it's you who is going to die today. A final death this time. One there is no coming back from."

"How can I die, when I have Death on my side?" He held out his hand, sickness flickering over his skin as he unleashed it upon me. I used a mix of air and light to block it and send it away from me, while darting to the side. He rapid-fired a dozen more arrows so fast I barely had a chance to deflect them, and then I went after him with my sword. His sickness leeched across my skin, making me feel tired and weak, but I fought it with everything I had.

At that moment, Lucifer opened the portal to Void with a tearing sound I'd never heard, like it had destroyed something in the fabric of the universe, like the realm itself was fighting this intrusion. The portal was a kaleidoscope of endlessly swirling glints of light moving dizzyingly against deep black, as hazes of gray mist drifted across it.

The portal was open—which meant I had to get Pestilence in it. As much as I hated to admit it, killing him was near impossible.

Or was it?

We all stood transfixed for a moment, staring at the portal, before springing back into action. Out of the corner of my eye I saw Lucifer fight against Death, trying to maneuver him toward the portal. I barely had time to notice though, as Pestilence dodged my every blow, not even breaking a sweat as I danced him across the plateau toward the portal. As we grew closer to it, he suddenly sprang at me, his face an abomination of evil as he gripped my shoulders and yanked me forward.

"I had thought death for you, Eve." Again, he used my first name, the one guaranteed to remind me of all we'd started as. The one he seemed to cling to as proof of his birthright. "But now I think you should be in the Void. Lost forever to your family."

Panic flared through me as he shoved me away from him and I fell toward the portal, but before I could save myself, Kassiel blocked me with his body. He helped me stand and said, "Go get him, Mom."

Then he flew off toward the cages, where Damien and Belial were already there trying to free our family. Aurora cried in her cage, and when I turned toward her, she waved her arms at me, her terrified eyes fixed on mine across the distance between us. She needed me, and it broke my heart to see her in such pain, but at least her brothers were there. They would keep her safe, I had no doubt. My heart burst with a mixture of anger, grief, pride, and love, making me even more determined to finally remove Adam from our lives.

I poured my emotions into my magic and made thorny vines grow up from the ground all around Adam, trusting my soldiers to keep Death's army from me while I focused. My plants wound around Adam's legs to hold him in place, and around his hands to trap his bow, then around the rest of his body until I could barely see him beneath the writhing green. But I didn't intend to suffocate him. Oh, no. For every painful death he'd given me he deserved so much more than mere deprivation of air. I squeezed my vines tight enough that a few bones cracked and the thorns dug deep into his flesh, and he cried out in pain.

But Pestilence was too strong, and he was already working to break free of my vines, tearing them off his body and making them wither and die with his sickness. That's when I called on my Famine powers to steal energy and power from him, dragging it out of his body and into me. I grew stronger, while he grew weaker. He tried to fight me with everything he had, but I was too much for him. I kept pulling and pulling, my hunger demanding more and more of Pestilence's essence, until I ripped the Elder God out of Adam entirely.

Adam staggered, his knees hitting the ground, his body weakened and battered by hosting Pestilence for so long. The Elder God hovered above me, a yellow spectral essence, a tainted cloud of putrid sickness. He spread his plagued fingers across the battlefield, searching for his next host, but I wasn't going to let that happen. I wrapped a swirling mass of air infused with light and darkness around him, then forced him into the portal. Pestilence screamed, a shrill, horrifying sound that made everyone on the battlefield feel queasy, as the portal to Void sucked him inside, like it too was greedy to lock him away.

Pestilence was gone—leaving only Adam behind. I was

his judge, jury, and executioner, and I'd tried him and found him wanting. Today, I was his reaper.

My entire world narrowed to just me and Adam. I stepped closer to him, clearing his body of the remaining vines that still clung to him, leaving grazes and cuts where their thorns had started to burrow. His body was covered in Pestilence's boils, his hair almost gone, his skin still a sickly color, though his Fallen powers tried their best to heal him. For a second I saw Gadreel, who I'd thought had been my friend, but who had tricked me for numerous lives. A bitter reminder of all that Adam had done.

He deserved to suffer for his sins.

"Eve... My Eve." His voice was weak, pleading, and it fueled the hate inside me. "I knew you'd come back to me. Heal me and we can be together finally."

"No." He didn't deserve any more words, and nothing I said would ever get through to him. He'd been a possessive, abusive husband when I was Eve, and after I'd left him, he'd only gotten worse. He'd never been able to let me go, his obsession carrying across multiple lives—thanks to Death's curse—for thousands of years. I had nothing in my heart for him but loathing for everything he'd stolen from me. I was literally a different person because of him. A different person again and again, always losing everything I held dear, then having to search for it over and over, knowing I would only lose it again.

I didn't plan to lose anything I loved ever again.

His face changed when he realized I wasn't going to

help him. "Whore," he yelled, followed by a dozen other obscenities, along with, "I'll kill you!"

"No, Adam. It's time for your final death."

I plunged my dark-and-light sword into his chest, slicing him open with a hard slash of my blade. His eyes widened at me, and he spat blood from his lips as he tried to fight back, but he wasn't strong enough to do anything to stop me. I felt his life force flicker, and it would have been so easy to steal his life and end his suffering, to feed my eternal hunger... But I did not.

Instead, I hit him with all of my rage and suffering, with all of the love I felt for my family, and the grief from when he'd taken me from them over and over. Light and darkness, air and vine, truth and hunger—all of my powers mixed together to rip him apart, atom by atom. His face became a mask of pain as he was torn asunder, his screams echoing across the battlefield, and then he was no more. My power devoured him, wiping him from existence entirely.

Adam was gone, and only I remained.

Our eternal battle was finally over.

34

LUCIFER

Even though I'd become War, my father still managed to overpower me. We wrestled like I was a child trying to move a man as I attempted to force him toward the Void portal. I was starting to think Death would be impossible to defeat. No one won their final war against him, though many had tried. How had I ever believed I might be the one exception?

I glimpsed Aurora behind him, now in Belial's arms but still reaching out toward us, her cries for her parents almost lost to the sound of battle. I couldn't let my father take my daughter away and raise her. No good came of having Death as a father figure. If anyone knew that, it was me.

"Oh, Lucifer," Death said. "You could have ruled all the worlds. I expected so much from you, my son. Instead you had to fall in love with that mortal woman. She made you weak."

Why was everyone always trying to convince me that

loving Hannah made me weaker? "No. Loving her has only made me stronger."

"You're wrong." Death shook his head at me, then gestured at Aurora and Belial. Undead immediately surrounded them, trying to tear my daughter from her brother's arms, but Damien blasted them all back with a burst of air. Zel, Lilith, and Cerberus, now freed by Kassiel, all leaped into the attack too, easily slicing down the skeletal attackers.

"You see," I said, turning back to my father. "Love wins."

But I'd been so distracted by the attack on my family that I hadn't noticed Death lunging toward me, and he managed to rip the Void key right out of my hand. Then he let out a guttural roar as he clenched it within his palm. Rays of light of every color shot out of it, before he closed his fist and shattered it into a million pieces. The portal to Void immediately closed behind him.

Fuck.

"Careless, Lucifer," Death chided. He wrapped his free hand around my neck and pinned me against him from behind. "Weak. Powerless. Useless. What a disappointment you are. Are you even my son? Or did that angel lie to me?"

"I guess I'm a mama's boy," I growled, as I grabbed his arm and flipped him over me. His back hit the ground hard, but then he slithered away, too fast for a mortal eye to see. But he wasn't getting away. I didn't know how I would stop him, but this had to end here. Maybe we could put him back in his tomb, which had to be behind him somewhere. There was a solution, I just had to find it.

I shot brilliant blue and red hellfire at him, but he always managed to escape it. I kept firing, pushing him back and back, toward the battle behind him. Then I released all my War powers and grabbed hold of every one of his undead soldiers, turning them against each other. Against him.

They swarmed his body, a writhing mass of bones and dead flesh, and I felt a deep sense of satisfaction at the sight. But then an ear-shattering roar burst out of Death and he shifted and grew, becoming a giant black wolf with glowing purple eyes and talons that turned the ground black around them. Fenrir's wolf form, now with an apocalyptic twist. Shit, maybe this really was Ragnarok.

Wolf-Death launched himself at me, and only the swift beat of my wings got me out of the way in time, though he did manage to rake a claw down my side. His mere touch leeched life out of me, and a deathly chill spread through my body. I sucked in air as I tried not to let Death overtake me. I was too strong to be so easily defeated—but how long could I last against this apocalyptic Death wolf?

Fingers curled around mine, and I looked into Hannah's face, smears of blood covering her cheeks, her hair coated with a fresh layer of fine gray ash. She'd managed to defeat Pestilence and Adam, and now she was by my side again, ready to face our other eternal enemy.

"Let's finish this." She sent a little life-giving energy into me, allowing me to fight off the last of Death's touch. "I can rip Death out of Fenrir. I just don't know what we'll do with him after that."

"I'll get him back in the tomb." Time for plan B. Or Q. Or whatever the fuck we were on at this point.

Hannah held her hands out, her body emitting a green glow as she sucked at Death's essence. He let out a skin-crawling howl that echoed throughout the battlefield, making everyone cover their ears. Then he charged her with his wolf body the size of a dump truck. I blasted him with hellfire so strong it knocked him back and set his fur on fire, but he stood up and shook it off, snapping at me with his massive fangs. Then a giant paw tried to rip me apart with its claws, but I flew around him and kept firing at him, distracting him while Hannah leeched away his life force. He grew weaker and weaker, the purple in his eyes dimming, his movements slowing down.

"I've nearly got him," Hannah ground out.

Purple essence seeped out slowly, unwillingly, from Fenrir's mouth, nose, and ears. I rushed to the base of the Sphinx, looking for Death's tomb—but it wasn't there.

Death suddenly released Fenrir's body, launching out of him, forming what looked like a spectral Grim Reaper in the air as it hovered over us. Fenrir shook out his wolf body, but then the two began to merge again—Death trying to return to its host. I shot all of my power into Death, holding him back with everything I had, but knew it wouldn't last. We had to kill Fenrir to sever the bond.

I quickly sought out my sons, even as I struggled to hold Death back. Belial was closest, and oddly enough, the one I trusted most with this task. I met his eyes and pointed at Fenrir, and he nodded as understanding settled over him.

Belial handed Aurora to Damien, unsheathed Morningstar in one quick movement, and plunged my old sword into Fenrir's throat. He acted quickly, bringing Morningstar down fast and sure, no lack of certainty and no hesitation. Fenrir couldn't even struggle, not as the light-infused blade cut him down, and he hit the ground hard. As he died, his body returned to his human state, looking small and broken on the ashen ground.

Fenrir was dead, but Death still remained. An Elder God with no tomb to lock him inside, and no Void portal to send him through. But he needed a body.

Death yanked himself free of my hold, and his essence began to float forward toward the person he'd already chosen as his new host. Death was the absence of indecision —and I knew his choice even before he got there.

Aurora.

"No!" I began to run toward my children. "Not her!"

Damien tried to rush away, carrying Aurora in his arms, but Death's skeletal army surrounded them from every side, with Theo at the head of them. Kassiel began to fight them off, and Olivia and her other mates joined him, but Death was too fast and too powerful.

Belial flew in front of Death's essence, shielding his siblings with his wings, his beautiful ombre feathers spread wide. He thrust Morningstar into the air, right into the middle of Death's essence, and the mist swirled around the blade, almost like a caress, spiraling to Belial's hand and arm like it was tasting him.

"Take me," Belial said. "Not the girl. She's only a child,

and still weak. You'll be too easy to defeat in her body. But I'm also your grandchild, and I'm almost as ancient as you are. With our power combined, we'll be unstoppable."

"Belial!" Hannah screamed. "Don't do this!"

I grabbed her hand and held her back. "No. He can do this. I have faith in him."

She looked at me like I was insane, but there was only one person here strong enough to contain Death. Hannah and I couldn't do it—we were already Elder Gods. It had to be Belial.

"But what if we lose him?" she whispered.

I squeezed her hand. "We won't."

"Why do you want this power?" Death asked Belial.

Our oldest son straightened up, his eyes blazing with fury. "To defeat my father once and for all and take my rightful place as Demon King."

His words were like a blow to my chest. After all we'd been through, did my son truly mean that? Had he done all of this just so he could have a chance to grab an Elder God's power? Had I really been so wrong about him?

Death cackled. "I like you, grandson. Perhaps my pedigree merely skipped a generation. Yes, you will make a fine host, at least until the girl is older. But I require a sacrifice."

Belial closed his eyes briefly, and then he looked at his mother, his gaze lingering on her as his face remained stoic. Then he turned his eyes upon me, and I saw the truth there, as if I'd had a touch of Hannah's power. Belial didn't want Death's power. He was only doing this to save his sister. He was doing this for *us*.

He looked at Aurora next, still in Damien's arms, and his jaw clenched. "Anything," he told Death.

"I require the sacrifice of your soul," Death rasped.

"Belial, no!" Hannah yelled, rushing forward to try to stop this somehow, but I wrapped my arms around her, wishing there was some other way to defeat Death and save my son. If Hannah and I could defeat the Elder Gods inside us, I had to believe Belial could do the same. Somehow.

Belial cast one last glance at us, as if saying goodbye, before he nodded at his grandfather. "Done."

Then I could only stare in horror as my son became Death, the destroyer of worlds.

35

HANNAH

As the last of the purple essence disappeared into my son, my tortured cry rang loud and harsh over the landscape and then echoed back, like the whole of Hell shared my grief. Behind us, the battle was still going on, but none of that mattered. All I cared about was that I was about to lose my son to Death.

I gripped Lucifer's hand, dragging him along with me as I crossed the distance between us and Belial, my wings bursting from my back when my legs didn't move fast enough. Damn it all. An Elder God couldn't have another one of my men. Death wouldn't take my son.

"Belial!" His name ripped from my throat. "Belial, you have to fight!"

Belial was kneeling in the dirt, shuddering with the aftermath of becoming Death, but then his head snapped up and his glowing eyes met mine. A horrible cackle escaped from his mouth, as purple magic slithered up and down his body, making his veins and bones glow from the inside out in a most horrifying way.

Theo landed in front of me, trying to block me from getting to my son, but Lucifer grabbed the gargoyle by the throat. He reached out with a tendril of darkness and picked up Morningstar, which had fallen when Belial had become Death, and yanked it into his hand. Without hesitation, Lucifer used the glowing sword to slice Theo's head off. When it was done, Lucifer tossed the gargoyle's body aside like it was a doll, then handed Morningstar to Kassiel and wiped his hands.

I couldn't even take satisfaction in the traitor's death, because all I could see was Belial, spreading his purple-tinged wings as he gazed across the battlefield at his undead army. When Belial had been a kid, he'd had horrible nightmares, and I would stroke his head and tell him everything was okay until he fell asleep again—but this was one monster I couldn't rid him of. If my sheer will had been enough, he would have returned to me immediately.

"Fight, Belial!" I called out. "Remember who you truly are!"

"Who I am?" He let out another horrible cackle. "I am Death. Belial is no more. He was weak, and now he is gone."

Lucifer clenched his fists. "No, he's not. You are Belial. Our first child. Our strongest son. I know you can fight this. Don't let him win."

Belial suddenly launched himself at Lucifer, wrapping

his hands around my mate's neck. Lucifer's eyes went wide as Death sucked the life out of him, making him go pale. "I am Death, and you will die!"

Instead of fighting him, Lucifer wrapped his arms around his son in a hug. "If you need to kill me, then so be it. If I could give my life to save you, I'd do it. I'd gladly sacrifice anything for you."

Death roared and released Lucifer, retreating away from us. He shook his head like he was confused, and I knew it was Belial trying to fight him off. All he needed was a little help from his family.

I gestured for my other sons to come close as I moved toward Death. Just like with War, I had to trust that Belial wouldn't hurt me. With Lucifer at my side, Kassiel moved to stand on the left, and Damien on the right. Aurora launched herself away from Damien and flew over to me, and I caught her in my arms, kissing her on the face, so relieved to have her back again. My entire family, reunited once again—and now we had to save one of our own.

"Belial, we love you," I said to him as he glared at us. "Focus on that. Focus on your family."

"Don't let past hurt dictate your actions, brother," Damien said.

"Please come back," Kassiel added. "We're all here waiting for you."

"Love is a lie," Belial said. "Love makes you weak. Love is *nothing*."

"That's Death talking," Lucifer said. "Not you."

"What would you know of love?" Belial asked, glaring at his father. "You neglected me as a child. You cast me out of Hell. You pretended I didn't exist for centuries. Now you speak to me of *love*? Where was your fucking love then?"

"I'm sorry." Lucifer's voice caught a little. "I've made many mistakes. I let my pride keep me from doing what was right. But I've always loved you, and I've always been proud of you, even if I was terrible at showing it. I promise I will do better going forward."

Belial responded by raising his arms, and his undead army charged toward us, plowing over our other soldiers to get to us. He was losing this battle against Death, and we had to do something. Something more. At first, I thought perhaps I could drain him of power, like I'd done to Adam and Fenrir, but then we'd be stuck with Death with no host and nowhere to put him. We had to get Belial to defeat Death instead.

I thought back to when Lucifer and I had defeated our Elder Gods, and how we'd called upon our opposite natures to fight back. With Famine, I'd used growth. With War, Lucifer had used peace. Which meant with Death, Belial had to use life. But how? He didn't possess that gift.

No, but I did.

Lucifer glanced at the oncoming horde of undead, but our soldiers were holding them off, for now anyway. Demeter and her fae warriors used air magic and elegant swords to keep them at bay. Gabriel and the other angels shot light and flew on shining wings over the battlefield.

Baal, Lilith, and Samael led the demons and Fallen forward, and among them I saw Zel slicing into shifters and gargoyles, and Cerberus tearing skeletons apart limb by limb. They were all giving us time, time enough to save our son.

I propped Aurora up on my hip, and then reached for the other's hands. They got the idea, and my family all linked hands as we circled around Death. He glared at us with purple eyes, but Belial held him back from attacking, as I'd known he would.

"What are you doing?" Death asked with a cold laugh. "You cannot stop me."

I released my Famine powers, but instead of taking energy, I gave it. I channeled life from my family and funneled it into Death, making him scream. Lucifer also released War's powers, but he reversed them, sending feelings of love and peace into our son instead of anger and hatred.

"Death will not take my son from me," I called out, as I felt Death fighting back, trying to quell my life-giving power. "I am a goddess of life, and my children carry that gift too. You cursed me to die again and again, but being reborn over and over only made me stronger. Now I give that power to Belial."

It was working. Death was weakening his hold on Belial. I saw my son's eyes shining through again. But I wasn't sure it would be enough, even with all of us sending life and love into him. Death was just too damn strong, like a black hole that sucked everything into it.

Then Aurora suddenly flew out of my grasp toward Belial, and I let out a little cry as I reached for her. It was too late though, and she landed in his arms, grabbing onto him. Belial lowered his head to her, his movements almost robotic as he caught his baby sister in his hands. I held my breath as I waited to see what would happen next. I was terrified, but I had faith too. Faith that Belial wouldn't hurt his sister. Faith that love would prevail.

"Yes, you will be an excellent host one day," Death said, and my hope faltered.

But then Aurora reached up to touch Belial's face, and they stared into each other's eyes and something passed between them. Power. Life. *Love.*

"Be be be," Aurora said, her voice clear even among the battlefield. Was she trying to say his name? He blinked at her, as if he wondered the same thing. She looked at him with pure baby adoration, her eyes shining with love for grumpy older brother, and that was enough to push him over the edge.

Belial threw his head back with a roar, and an inner war waged inside him, one we could do nothing more to fight. It seemed to last for an eternity, but then Belial prevailed, and all the purple glow around him vanished back inside his body. He staggered, and I rushed forward to take Aurora from him, while Lucifer caught him in his arms.

Belial coughed. "He's... He's gone."

"Yes, my father is gone," Lucifer said. "But Death remains. You are an Elder God now."

"How do you feel?" Kassiel asked.

"Fucking great," Belial said sarcastically, as he pulled away from Lucifer and stood on his own.

"How is this possible?" Damien asked.

I gave a little shrug as I smiled at my sons. "Love is stronger than death."

Lucifer nodded. "Yes, love persists, even after someone is gone. It's the reason we grieve someone, or smile at the memory of them. It was the one thing Death hated more than anything else, and the reason he cursed me and Hannah all those years ago. Love is the only thing he could never kill."

"That's lovely, but would you mind stopping your undead horde before they kill my grandmother?" Damien asked, tilting his head toward the battle behind us.

"Oh. Right." Belial lifted his hands in silent command and the undead all fell, their bones collapsing to the ground or becoming dust once again.

Once they were gone, the battle was over. The remaining shifters, imps, and other traitors surrendered, and we could all breathe a little sigh of relief at last.

I drew Aurora into my arms and wrapped her tightly to my chest, dropping kisses into her wisps of blond hair. "Good girl," I whispered. "Did you see what you did? You saved your brother." I hugged her to me again and her fingers batted my cheek. I turned my head to kiss her little hands as Lucifer gathered us both against him, wrapping us in his arms and his wings.

He released a sigh and bent to kiss Aurora's head. "You're both incredible."

Aurora giggled and reached for his feathers. He let her touch them for a few moments before he took her from me, and his wings folded away. I went straight to Belial next.

"Are you all right?" I asked, wrapping my arms around him and giving him a long, tight squeeze. I'd almost lost him today.

"I'm fine," he said, slowly pulling out of my pincer hold. "Thanks to you."

He said that, but I was his mother, and I knew it was a lie. Something about him was different. Colder. Emptier.

But of course he was different. He was a god now.

Lucifer walked over next and clasped Belial on the shoulder, while still holding Aurora. "I knew you could do it."

"Did you?" Belial asked, genuinely surprised.

He nodded. "I never had any doubt you would find your way back to us."

"Be be be," Aurora said, and Belial gave her something that was almost a smile as he held out a hand to her.

"But you sacrificed your soul," Kassiel said. "What does that mean?"

Damien tapped his lips. "Father sacrificed his memories, but those were returned. Could Belial's soul be restored too?"

I shook my head. "I don't know. I hope so."

Lucifer put an arm around my waist. "We're all here.

Together again. If there's a way to save Belial's soul, we'll find it."

Belial rolled his eyes. "I'm fine. Really."

He did seem all right, so it was hard to tell what exactly losing his soul had done to him. I prayed it was nothing, and that he would be able to move forward with his life—now with a bit more power. Either way, I knew I'd be back in the library looking for answers as soon as we returned home. That was what I did, after all.

A pale horse suddenly galloped over to us and bowed its head to Belial, who looked surprised by this turn of events. He was a Horsemen now, like Lucifer and I were. But there were only three of us on Earth now, and perhaps that meant the threat of the apocalypse was over. After all, all the prophecies said there had to be four.

As Hell quieted down around us, I leaned against Lucifer as we gazed across the battlefield at the aftermath of our apocalyptic war. A war we'd somehow won, despite all odds. Marcus and some other angels were healing the injured. Romana and Azazel had rounded up the remaining enemy soldiers and subdued them, while Cerberus growled and kept the prisoners in line. I spotted Demeter among the fae, adjusting her armored crown. Everyone I loved had come to fight this battle with us, and we'd prevailed.

A huge wave of relief washed over me as I turned toward Lucifer, who was still holding Aurora. I wrapped my arms around the both of them, holding them close. We were free. Free of Death's curse. Free of Adam's threat. Free to have a normal life. Well, as normal as life could be when it consisted of angels, demons, fae, babies who could fly, and three-headed hellhounds. Not to mention a couple Horsemen of the Apocalypse.

"We did it," Lucifer said, before pressing a kiss to my lips. "We won."

I nodded, tears of happiness filling my eyes. "Let's go home and celebrate."

36

LUCIFER

Hannah and I entered the conference room in The Celestial, which we'd decided would still be our base of operations for our empire, even though we made our home in southern California now. Las Vegas was the main hub for demons on Earth and that wouldn't change. After all, with the internet and a private jet we could rule from anywhere. Damn, I loved this century.

My queen and I took our places at both heads of the table and I let my gaze slowly fall on each of the people in front of me. It had been three weeks since we'd stopped Death and Pestilence, and I'd called a meeting of Archdemons, both new and old. I had some changes to make to prepare for the future of our people, to usher them into a new era.

Lilith sat to my left, fully recovered after her kidnapping and looking as lovely as ever. On my right was Baal, wearing a suit that looked like it has been made during Victorian times. Next to him was Romana, across from Samael, both of them looking stoic. Then down by Hannah was Valefar, representing the dragons for the first time, and Bastet, the leader of the feline shifters, and the newest Archdemon in our ranks. She'd been quick to pledge her loyalty to me after Fenrir's death, swearing her people would root out the corruption and bring the other shifter clans in line. Since the insurrection had mostly involved wolves and bears, I was willing to let her try. Besides, she'd hated Fenrir for thousands of years, and was thrilled to take his place—and that was enough to keep her loyal. For now, anyway.

The final seat at the table stood empty. No Archdemon had been chosen for the imps yet, and from what I'd heard, their ranks were in chaos. One of the many things on today's agenda.

"Thank you for joining us today," I said. "We have much to discuss."

"Yes, big changes are coming," Hannah said, as she took her seat with a smile.

The Archdemons bristled and glanced between each other. "Are the rumors true?" Romana asked. "Are you stepping down?"

A hearty laugh erupted from me. "No, of course not. Why would anyone think that?"

The demons settled down at those words. Immortals didn't like change. They tended to be stuck in their ways, even if those ways were outdated and it was obvious that a new way would be better for them. Of course, change was necessary for the survival of our people. I'd been doing a lot of thinking over the last few weeks, and realized that was where I'd failed as a ruler before. I'd been either too hesitant to change, or I'd embraced it too hastily. But now I had Hannah ruling with me to help find the right balance.

I slowly sat in my executive chair like it was a throne, my back straight, letting my hands languish on the armrests. "The first business on the agenda is a promotion. Samael, please rise."

"Yes, my lord?" He reluctantly stood up, towering over the rest of the table.

"Samael, Hannah and I are pleased to announce that you are now officially an Archdemon, representing the Fallen."

"I... I don't understand," he said. "The Fallen don't have an Archdemon."

"They do now," Hannah said with a big smile for her friend.

I nodded. Until now I'd acted as both Demon King and leader of the Fallen, but it was time to delegate more. Plus, Samael deserved a promotion for everything he did for us. "It's something I should have done centuries ago."

"Agreed," Lilith said, giving Samael a sultry smile. "You've basically had the job all these years anyway, Sam. It's high time you were recognized for it."

"Thank you," Samael said, bowing his head, and the other Archdemons offered their congratulations. "I will do everything in my power to serve the Fallen as their leader."

"I know you will," I said. "And I hope this will address another issue—the belief among some that Fallen are not true demons, or that I favor them over other demon races. That is false. We are all creatures of the night and children of Hell, and Hannah and I will rule over all demons equally and impartially."

This was something Mammon had brought up as a reason why he was trying to overthrow me, and after speaking with some of the other Archdemons privately over the last few weeks, I'd discovered it was a larger problem than I'd realized. I hoped that by making Samael the Archdemon of the Fallen it would solidify him as their leader and representative, and allow me to treat all the demonic races as equal subjects. After all, I wasn't really Fallen, not anymore, and neither was my queen.

I steepled my fingers on the table as we moved on to the next order of business. "As for the imps, we will give them one more week, and if an Archdemon is not named, we will choose one for them. Does anyone have a person they would like to nominate?"

"That won't be necessary," a lilting voice said from the doorway. Audible gasps went up around the room as our unexpected guest strode into the room. I hadn't seen the man in hundreds of years, and though he could change his appearance at will, I recognized that cocky swagger immediately—Loki.

Today he wore wavy black hair, cheekbones that could cut glass, and mischievous green eyes, with his trademark crooked smile. An ancient imp, he was the cousin of Nemesis, and also the father of Fenrir, who had taken after his wolf mother in his powers. Was Loki here to swear his loyalty—or here for revenge?

I rose to my feet, preparing myself in case he launched an attack. "Welcome, Loki. It's been a long time."

"Where have you been all these years?" Bastet asked, with a toss of her dark brown hair. The way she said it made me think they had once been an item.

"Oh, you know. Here and there." Loki waved a hand with a mysterious smile. "I've been hanging out, doing my own thing, but it seems I'm needed now. I'm here as the new Archdemon of the imps, and ready to swear my loyalty to good ol' Lucifer and his lovely queen." He winked at Hannah as he said that, and I barely held back a growl.

Instead, I raised an eyebrow at Hannah, silently asking her if he was speaking the truth. She studied him closely, no doubt reading his aura, and then nodded to me.

"Oh good, I see I have your approval." Loki swept into an elaborate bow before us. "I am your humble servant, my king and queen. I pledge my loyalty to you, and swear to serve as your Archdemon to my best capabilities."

I didn't like this, not one bit. Loki was the most famous trickster of all time, and damn crafty too. If he'd emerged after centuries there had to be a reason, one we might not know for many years—and I didn't believe for one second it was because the imps needed him. But what was that saying —keep your friends close, and your enemies closer?

I flashed him one of my own charming smiles. "We're so pleased to have you with us. Please, take a seat."

Everyone's eyes were on Loki as he draped himself across the chair. "With pleasure."

Hannah cast a warm smile around the table and drew everyone's gaze back to her when she spoke. "Now that the Archdemon issue is settled, we can move on to the next thing on our agenda. Hell."

"What about it?" Baal asked.

I sat back in my chair. "We're going to start rebuilding it."

That got everyone's attention.

"Do you plan for us to return there?" Valefar asked. It was another thing his father, Mammon, had wanted. After speaking with the other Archdemons, it seemed many of my subjects also wanted that—while many others had absolutely no desire to leave Earth.

"Eventually, yes," Hannah said. "Once we've rebuilt some of Hell and determined it is habitable again, we'll open passage to any demon who wants to return there. We know many have made their homes on Earth and will not want to leave, but there are others who long to return to our old realm."

"We'd like to set up a team with representatives from all seven demon races to lead this project," I said. "Please choose five of your people whom you think would be best for this task and report back by the end of the month."

Baal gave me a respectful nod. "This will go a long way into reuniting our people."

"Will it?" Lilith asked. "Or will it set up another divide of Earth versus Hell demons?"

"We'll try to prevent that from happening by allowing

demons to pass freely between the two realms," Hannah said.

Valefar stroked his chin. "My people would approve of that. Hell is much safer for my dragons than Earth, but with our numbers so few, we also need to be in this realm to reproduce and rebuild our race."

Bastet leaned toward me and asked, "But will you be ruling the demons on Earth or the ones in Hell?"

"Both." I leveled a gaze at anyone who might try to challenge me, then gave them another disarming smile. "Although I won't be able to do it without my Archdemons. I'll need all of you more than ever. I see a bright future for our people—but it will take all of us working together to usher the demons into the next era."

Loki gave me a slow clap and then grinned at the others. "Well, I don't know about the rest of you, but I'm sold. Sign me up, Old Scratch."

I tried not to grit my teeth at that old nickname and instead kept my smile on my face. "Excellent. Now, if there are matters that any of you would like to discuss, the floor is open."

Bastet began speaking about her plans to deal with the various shifter packs, and the others chimed in with some ideas or questions. As the meeting went on, I found my eyes drifting back to Hannah, watching her command the room with ease. She'd changed so much, it was hard to believe she'd once been the innocent woman who'd come to my door asking me for a favor. My Eve. My Persephone. My Hannah.

Her eyes met mine, and she gave me a smile that was just for me, filled with love and respect. She was my equal. My mate. My wife.

My queen.

37

HANNAH

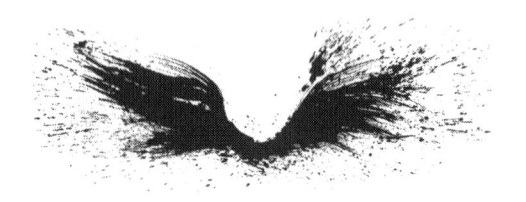

I stretched and rolled over in bed, not really wanting to be awake but being awake all the same. Not that I needed sleep, of course. I just liked it. It made me feel a little less...godlike.

"Good morning." Lucifer's voice was warm and full of promise, and as his hand skimmed my hip, I suddenly didn't mind being awake at all. He kissed my neck, his soft hair brushing my cheek, before I'd even opened my eyes. I had a feeling he'd been up for hours. Unlike me, Lucifer couldn't be bothered to sleep.

"Morning," I murmured back, luxuriating in his touch and warm mouth as he nibbled his way along my jaw.

The house was so quiet. Peaceful.

My eyes flew open. "Aurora."

Lucifer's hand was against my cheek, his eyes looking into mine. "She's still asleep. Just be here with me." He resumed his gentle nibbling as his hand swept my hip again, then rested over my ribs so his thumb pressed softly against the underside of my breast.

I wanted to offer him encouragement, but couldn't tear my thoughts away from a sudden mental onslaught of party plans, caterers, guests, and a one-year-old birthday girl. There would be time for Lucifer later. I'd make sure of it.

"As much I'd like to continue this, I have shit to do," I said with a sigh.

Lucifer laughed at my eloquent words. "What shit?"

"Party shit," I clarified. "Aurora only turns one once, and people are coming here expecting a party, not to join us in our bedroom for the world's most powerful orgy."

His eyes flickered with interest. "An orgy? How very old school. You know I'm down for it."

"Maybe some other time." I laughed and pressed my palm to his chest as I lifted away from his body. "I call the shower first."

I paused for a fraction of a second, knowing what I'd hear next.

"Let's conserve water," Lucifer drawled, as he stood in all his naked glory.

I grinned. Fine, maybe the party shit could wait a little bit longer.

I looked out over our friends and family the same way I had after the final battle with Pestilence and Death, but this time the air around me rang with laughter rather than the aftermaths of battle. Today everyone we loved was gathered to celebrate Aurora's first birthday, and I couldn't be happier. Tents had been set up around our garden once again with outdoor couches and tables, and a huge buffet stood at one side, along with an open bar, naturally. Lucifer wouldn't have it any other way.

I glanced around for my daughter, and spotted her with Demeter. Of course. Demeter had perhaps the greatest patience for holding Aurora's hand while she tottered along, trying so hard to walk. Round and round the garden, her chunky little thighs carrying her forward, while her wings tried to lift her up.

Balloons waved here and there in the air, and Aurora reached for them, flying up, up, up, then sending them bouncing away with her clumsy attempts to capture them. Demeter caught her and smiled, kissing her cheeks, doting her with grandmotherly love. Demeter was still a bit frosty with me and Lucifer, but she had nothing but warmth for Aurora.

Behind her, Lilith sat with Brandy and Asmodeus, holding little Isaac as he bounced on her lap. She looked positively smitten with her own grandchild, while Samael, Baal, and Gabriel chatted beside her. Olivia, Lilith's daughter with Gabriel, came to sat with her, taking the baby from her arms with a smile. Callan, Marcus, and Bastien dropped onto a table nearby, and I smiled at this huge family Brandy had somehow gotten herself involved with. I bet she'd had no idea what she was getting into when she fell for

Asmodeus, but judging by her smile and the love her son was getting, she didn't mind one bit.

They were my family too, of course. Olivia was tied to my son and my nephew, making us all connected. I wouldn't have it any other way.

"Nice party," Zel said, draping an arm over my shoulder. "Am I allowed to give Aurora her daggers yet?"

I sighed and laughed, all at once. "Not for another few years."

"Damn. I was so looking forward to beginning her training."

I leaned against my best friend. "She's still too young, but in a few years you can teach her everything you know. I can't imagine a better mentor for her."

Zel grumbled. "Fine, I guess I can wait a little longer. At least until she's walking properly."

"Thank you." I studied her face, searching for signs of sadness. "But is this enough for you? Are you happy here with us?"

Zel shrugged. "I'm content. I have purpose. I'm with people I love. That's enough for me."

I nodded slowly, but hoped one day Zel would be able to find love again, even though her mate had died. Was it possible to have a second fated mate? I wasn't sure, but at this point I'd settle for Zel meeting a nice woman who made her smile.

I searched the party for my sons, and spotted Damien and Kassiel sitting together at the far edge of the tents while drinking beers. Relaxing together, trading quips, and rubbing Cerberus's many heads as he tried to steal the cheese off their plates. But where was Belial?

I spotted him standing by himself, gazing out at the ocean. He had his hands shoved in the pockets of his jeans, and the wind whipped at his dark hair. My heart clenched at the sight of him, worried something was wrong, but then Lucifer joined him there and the two of them spoke softly to each other. Whatever they said was lost on the wind before it reached my ears, but I was just happy they were speaking again.

Belial still seemed different, but he swore that he was fine, and I wasn't sure what—if anything—I could do for him at this point. Like me and Lucifer, he had to learn how to deal with being an Elder God, with Death being a permanent part of him now, and everything that entailed. It wasn't easy, but Lucifer and I were there for him if he had any problems. As for the matter of his missing soul...well, I still wasn't sure what that meant, but I would find out. When Lucifer and I put our minds to something, nothing could stop us.

As I continued to watch the party guests, Lucifer moved behind me, resting his hands on my hips and pressing a kiss to my neck. "What are you thinking about?"

"Fate," I said. "Life. Love."

He nuzzled my neck. "Sex?"

A short laugh escaped me. "Is that all you think about?"

Lucifer's hand had already drifted to my ass. "When you wear skimpy little dresses like that, yes."

"Later," I said, a promise I intended to keep. "After the guests have gone."

"I'm holding you to that."

True to his word, Lucifer found me out on the balcony later that night. The party was finished, Aurora was in bed, and I was staring at the ocean, much like Belial had done earlier.

"Still thinking about love?" Lucifer asked, as he moved toward me. He was shirtless now, wearing only black slacks that fit his body perfectly.

"With you? Always."

"You did make me a promise." His hands skimmed along my sides, as he raised up the dress I was wearing to expose my thighs. "I had an idea... Something we haven't done in many years."

My eyebrows darted up at that. "What would that be?"

He yanked the dress off me, while at the same time his shadow magic ripped off everything I'd been wearing underneath. Then he dropped his own trousers, freeing his impressive cock.

He took my hand as his black wings stretched out behind him. "Come with me, love."

My own silver wings extended, and together we flew up into the night, both of us completely naked, though Lucifer's shadow magic kept us hidden from anyone who happened to look up. Once we were hovering above our estate, I took it all in, enjoying the view of our home. Our palace on Earth.

But that wasn't why Lucifer had brought me up here. He drew me toward him, his wings spread wide behind him, and then his mouth crashed down on mine while his hands found my thighs again. His kiss was rough and demanding, as were his fingers as he moved across my skin. My desire immediately spiked as I realized what he had in mind.

I brought my hands to Lucifer's shoulders and his muscles flexed and moved beneath my touch as he continued to trail kisses over me. Wet, open-mouthed kisses down my neck. A hint of teeth. The flick of his tongue over my collarbone, and the soft caress of his fingers over my breasts, spiraling my nipple until it hardened and I arched against him.

"I see I have your attention now," he said with a smirk.

"Mmhmm." I threaded my fingers into his hair as his lips closed over my nipple before he sucked it into his mouth. Then he moved his ministrations to my other breast and his cock rested hard and heavy against my thigh. I grinned as he drew back and forth across my skin a little. "I see I'm not the only one at attention."

"If only you knew how you've tormented me over the centuries. Able to make my body respond with just a glance, or the sound of your breathing, your fragrance lingering in a room after you've left..."

"I know exactly what you mean." I tugged on his hair, wanting his mouth back on mine, while my wings flapped slowly behind us to help keep us aloft. The wind blew lightly against us, the night air cold against my skin, but I knew Lucifer's touch would keep me warm.

He obliged me, his lips widening into a grin before they captured mine and his tongue slipped into my mouth, slow and smooth and seeking something, but in no hurry. Taking his time because we suddenly had plenty of it. No emergencies, no one to fight, no one in danger.

I kissed him back, reveling in our freedom, and I worked my hand beneath his body and mine, tracing the valleys between his muscles, then down to stroke his cock, which hardened even more as he drew a sharp breath.

"Tease."

"You wouldn't have me any other way." I laughed and pressed a kiss to his throat.

"I'd have you every other way, Hannah." He gripped my legs and spread them around his hips, while his black wings beat behind him. "All the ways. And I'll have you now."

I wrapped my arms around his neck and ground against him. "Promises, promises."

While we hovered in the air, he rolled his hips forward, and the head of his cock probed between my folds. I tightened my legs around him as he filled me completely, making me cry out with the perfection of it. I dropped my head back as I savored the feel of him inside me. The closest two people could get. Two mates, joined together as one, our souls intertwined as much as our bodies were. We were the king and queen of night, and we consumated our love amongst the stars.

Lucifer's hands were on my hips as he began thrusting

into me, using his wings to propel him forward with more momentum. He started out slow and easy, hard and deep, but then I used my own wings to push back against him, making our pace speed up. He grunted and suddenly flew up higher, impaling me on his cock as we became one with the night, reaching for the moon, and I held onto his shoulders and let him take me for a ride.

We shot through the air, moving faster than should have been possible, our bodies joined together. Fucking in the air was like nothing else I'd ever experienced, a true give and take, and every thrust was met with a flutter of wings to keep us aloft. Lucifer's feathers brushed against me, their delicate touch the perfect contrast to his demanding movements. His fingers were almost bruising against me as he moved my body against him, hitting just the right spot every time.

We had sex as only gods could, pumping stronger and faster than any mortal could take, our pleasure heightened by the power coursing through us and the way our wings kissed the air as they moved. I reached up to stroke his feathers, and he let out a loud groan.

"Fuck, Hannah. Come for me." His breaths came faster as he pummeled me. "I want to feel you squeeze my cock as you lose control."

"When I'm ready." I wanted to drag this out as long as possible, but I couldn't stop the pleasure building inside me. He was too good. He was touching all the right places, and soon all I could do was gasp and moan as he took me harder and faster. His hands rested on my ass, kneading me there, demanding I follow his orders.

"I said, come for me," he growled, as his cock plunged deep.

I arched back against him, my wings flaring out as the orgasm flooded me with heat and power. Lucifer groaned too as I tightened up around his cock, my legs still squeezing around his hips, unwilling to let him go until he'd fully released himself inside me. He pushed upward one last time as we clung to one another, our wings barely keeping us afloat as overwhelming pleasure made us lose control of ourselves.

"I love you," he said, burying his face in my neck. "Across every lifetime. For all eternity."

"I love you too. Always."

We pulled apart so we could do a few lazy laps over our home, but our hands stayed intertwined the entire time. As I gazed over at my mate, his eyes bright under the twinkling stars and soft moonlight, all I felt was love and peace. Against all odds, Lucifer and I had found each other across hundreds of lifetimes, and managed to defeat the curse that kept separating us. We overcame Death, and finally took down Pestilence. We no longer had to live in fear of what Adam might do to us, or to our children. We were free.

Most importantly, we'd brought our family back together—and we'd resolved to never let it be torn apart again, no matter what threats we might face in the future. Whatever happened, we were ready for the next chapter of our story.

It was time to live.

ABOUT THE AUTHOR

Elizabeth Briggs is the *New York Times* bestselling author of paranormal and fantasy romance. She graduated from UCLA with a degree in Sociology and has worked for an international law firm, mentored teens in writing, and volunteered with dog rescue groups. Now she's a full-time geek who lives in Los Angeles with her family and a pack of fluffy dogs.

Visit Elizabeth's website: www.elizabethbriggs.net

Printed in Great Britain
by Amazon